Where could Sue be? Elizabeth wondered if she had staged another traumatic diversion to get Jeremy back. *Or what if her suicide attempt was successful this time?* Elizabeth thought in consternation. She looked up at the branch of a majestic oak tree and pictured Sue swinging lightly in the wind, hanging from the branch with a noose tied around her neck. The leaves crackled as she stepped on them and Elizabeth looked around wildly, exhaling sharply. *Or what if some psychotic killer found her and strangled her?* worried Elizabeth. Elizabeth felt her way through the brush with caution, expecting to stumble upon the body at any moment. She shivered and wrapped her overcoat tightly around her.

DEATH THREAT

Written by
Kate William

Created by
FRANCINE PASCAL

BANTAM BOOKS
NEW YORK · TORONTO · LONDON · SYDNEY · AUCKLAND

RL 6, age 12 and up

DEATH THREAT

A Bantam Book / November 1994

Sweet Valley High® is a registered trademark of Francine Pascal
Conceived by Francine Pascal
Produced by Daniel Weiss Associates, Inc.
33 West 17th Street
New York, NY 10011
Cover art by Bruce Emmett

ISBN: 0-553-56232-0

Published simultaneously in the United States and Canada

Bantam Books are published by Bantam Books, a division of Bantam Doubleday Dell Publishing Group, Inc. Its trademark, consisting of the words "Bantam Books" and the portrayal of a rooster, is Registered in U.S. Patent and Trademark Office and in other countries. Marca Registrada. Bantam Books, 1540 Broadway, New York, New York 10036.

PRINTED IN THE UNITED STATES OF AMERICA

OPM   0 9 8 7 6 5 4 3 2 1

To Jonathan David Rubin

Chapter 1

"Sue has disappeared? What do you mean?" Elizabeth Wakefield demanded of Jeremy Randall as he stood at the Wakefield front door with a stricken look on his face.

It was two o'clock in the morning on Sunday after the eventful Halloween party at the Project Nature cabin. Elizabeth had just driven her inconsolable twin sister, Jessica, home from the party and was trying to comfort her in the cozy Wakefield kitchen. During the party Jessica had discovered Jeremy in the arms of his former fiancée, Sue Gibbons, in the woods. She had charged into the cabin to find Elizabeth, insisting between sobs that they leave immediately. A distraught Jessica had wept all the way home, lamenting the loss of her one true love.

Elizabeth felt terrible for her sister, but she had to bite her tongue to keep from saying "I told you so." Jessica had fallen in love with Jeremy while he

1

was engaged to Sue, and they had dated in secret for weeks. Elizabeth had known all along that a man who was two-timing his fiancée was bad news. And now it looked as if he was two-timing his *new* fiancée—Jessica—as well. So, as she had done with Sue, Elizabeth was playing the role of the shoulder to cry on.

"It's not fair!" Jessica wailed, breaking out into a fresh round of sobs. She slumped down into her chair and sniffed into a pink tissue. "Just when we finally get the chance to be together, Sue has to come along and ruin everything! That manipulative little monster, that scheming little—" Jessica's voice choked up.

Elizabeth placed a cup of steaming hot chocolate in front of Jessica and pushed a wooden bowl of buttery popcorn toward her. "Here, drink some of this," coaxed Elizabeth, handing the hot chocolate to her sister. "It will make you feel better."

"I'll never feel better," declared Jessica dramatically, cupping the steamy mug in her hands. Fresh tears clouded her eyes and trickled down her face into the hot chocolate. "How could he do that to me? How could he betray me like—hey, what's that?" Jessica asked, sitting up suddenly.

As Elizabeth listened to the usual night sounds of the Wakefield household, she could hear a faint knocking on the front door. Jessica's eyes lit up with hope.

Oh, no! Elizabeth thought in alarm, overcome with a protective feeling for her love-struck sister. If it was Jeremy, she wasn't going to let him sweet-talk Jessica into forgiving him. "Don't worry, I'll take

2

care of it," Elizabeth assured her, jumping up.

If that two-timing louse has the nerve to show up here now, I am going to give him a piece of my mind, thought Elizabeth as she marched resolutely into the foyer. Maybe Jessica's actions hadn't been particularly admirable lately, but all the same—nobody got away with cheating on her twin sister.

Elizabeth peered through the peephole of the solid front door, and sure enough, there was the rat himself. She flung the door open and fixed Jeremy with a steely stare. "If you're here to make excuses to my sister, you can just forget it, because she's had it with you!" proclaimed Elizabeth in her haughtiest tone. As Jeremy opened his mouth to respond, Elizabeth slammed the door in his face.

"No, wait!" Jessica called from the kitchen, scrambling out of her chair and careening around the corner. "What are you doing?" she hissed as she slid into the foyer. "He's come back for me!"

Elizabeth stared at her sister in amazement. What had happened to the old Jessica, the headstrong Jessica, who set the rules in the game of love and made sure everybody else played by them? In matters of the heart Jessica had always had boys wrapped around her little finger. But now it looked as if she had turned into a spineless slave to love.

Jeremy knocked softly on the door again. Jessica gave her sister a reproving look and pulled the door open. The sight of Jeremy's chiseled face surrounded by a halo of golden hair made her melt. For a moment she didn't care that she had just caught Jeremy with Sue. Ever since Jessica had met Jeremy on the

3

beach the previous summer, she had decided that nothing would stand in the way of her love for him—not even Sue Gibbons, who happened to be Jeremy's fiancée as well as the Wakefields' houseguest. Sue's mother, Nancy Gibbons, had recently died of a rare blood disease. She had been Mrs. Wakefield's roommate at college and a cherished friend. As a tribute to her dear old friend, Alice Wakefield had invited Jeremy and Sue to Sweet Valley. Sue had always dreamed of having a California wedding, and Alice Wakefield was determined to make that dream come true.

But Jessica Wakefield had been equally determined to prevent that dream from becoming a reality. In the midst of all the wedding preparations, Jessica had made sure that Jeremy's mind wasn't on his bride-to-be, but on her blond hostess. Jessica had fallen head over heels in love with Jeremy, and they had pursued their love for each other through clandestine moments stolen together. Finally, as they sneaked away one evening in Jeremy's car to go to Miller's Point, a romantic parking spot in Sweet Valley, Jessica had put her foot down. "Jeremy, we can't always be running away like this," she had declared. And Jeremy had agreed.

So Jeremy had decided to call off the wedding. But just when he approached Sue to give her the bad news, she gave him even worse news—she, too, had the same rare blood disease her mother had died of and only had a few years to live. Unable to desert her in her time of need, Jeremy had resolved to make Sue's final years her happiest ones.

4

Jeremy had bought Sue's story hook, line, and sinker, but Jessica was skeptical. In Jessica's mind Sue's only terminal illness was a severe case of love-sickness. Jessica resolved then and there not to let Sue stand in the way of her destiny. So at the wedding, when the priest had asked if there was any reason why Jeremy and Sue shouldn't be married, Jessica had provided one. "Jeremy's in love with me," she had declared, and Jeremy had confirmed her sentiment.

The result was pandemonium. In the wake of the failed wedding, Sue had broken down, falling into a deep depression, and attempted suicide. But it turned out that Jessica's suspicions had been right all along. Sue had invented her terminal illness as a means to avoid losing Jeremy. And even though the ensuing weeks following the disastrous event were traumatic for Sue, she had eventually adjusted to the situation—and to the news that Jeremy and Jessica had gotten engaged themselves.

Now Jessica looked up at Jeremy with newfound determination. After all they had been through, she wasn't going to let Sue drive them apart. *After all, what's a little kiss in the grand scheme of things?* she told herself. All that mattered was that she and Jeremy were together, just as they were meant to be. Jessica felt an irresistible urge to throw herself at him, as if a magnetic pull were exerting a force on her heart. She gazed up into his eyes, prepared to run into his arms. But suddenly she registered a look on his face that she had never seen before: fear.

"It's Sue," Jeremy said, his face ashen. "She's disappeared."

"OK, tell us the whole story," said Elizabeth when the three of them were seated at the kitchen table.

"Well, there's not much to tell," Jeremy said, looking haggard. "Sue disappeared from the party right after you and Jessica left."

"What do you mean, 'disappeared'?" Elizabeth said.

"Vanished, vamoosed, not a trace of her," said Jeremy with a snap of his fingers.

Remembering Sue's botched suicide attempt, Elizabeth felt a coil of fear in her stomach. What if Sue had tried again, but this time successfully? "OK, start at the beginning," Elizabeth said. "What were you and Sue doing together in the first place?"

"Well, I was at the party when Sue came up and said she had something urgent to discuss with me," began Jeremy. "I asked her if it could wait, but she was insistent, saying that her life depended on it." A chill traveled down Elizabeth's spine at Jeremy's words.

"So we went outside, and—"

"But why did you go into the woods?" interrupted Jessica. Elizabeth was glad to see that her sister was finally regaining some of her old assertiveness.

"She insisted on going outside where we could talk in private," explained Jeremy. "When we were in the woods, she said she couldn't live without me. I had told her in no uncertain terms that it was over between us, but she couldn't seem to accept it. She broke down and began crying hysterically. And then she threw her arms around me."

6

"And kissed you passionately—?" Jessica asked, confusion evident in her voice.

Jeremy nodded, turning imploring eyes on her. "You've got to believe me," he said, speaking in an urgent tone. "She threw herself at me, and you showed up before I could pull away." Jeremy looked deep into Jessica's eyes. "Jess, I was just trying to comfort her. You know there's nothing between me and Sue—and there hasn't been for a long time."

"I believe you, honey," said Jessica, taking his hand. Her eyes were shining. "Remember—nothing can get in the way of our love." Jessica was elated at the news that Jeremy and Sue weren't back together. She ran the information through her mind: it was all a misunderstanding; Sue had just flung herself at her old fiancée; Jeremy was comforting her only because he was so noble and self-sacrificing. It all made perfect sense. Sue was desperate to get Jeremy back. And who could blame her? Jessica gazed into Jeremy's deep coffee-brown eyes. But Sue was naive, thought Jessica with a feeling of superiority, to think she could get in the way of their love. Didn't she realize that true love always persevered?

As Elizabeth noted the tender look that passed between Jessica and Jeremy, she experienced a sick feeling in the pit of her stomach. Elizabeth hadn't approved of Jeremy ever since he'd expressed an interest in her sister. Jeremy was twenty-three years old, much too old for a girl of sixteen. And he seemed to make a practice of cheating on his girlfriends. Even though Jeremy had provided an excuse for his actions that evening, somehow his story didn't wash.

7

Elizabeth couldn't understand why Jessica was being so gullible.

As she watched Jessica cuddle up to Jeremy, Elizabeth marveled at how different she and her sister were. Despite their identical appearances, from their shoulder-length golden-blond hair to their sparkling blue-green eyes to the matching dimple in their left cheek, she and Jessica were completely different in character. Jessica thrived on fun and adventure, always ready to go to the latest party, to spend the day on the beach gossiping and perfecting her tan, or to hit the mall with her friends. While Elizabeth enjoyed having a good time just as much as her sister, she preferred quieter pursuits. She could often be found curled up in an armchair with her journal or taking a walk on the beach with her boyfriend, Todd Wilkins. Even their activities reflected their different personalities, mused Elizabeth. Jessica was an active member of the twins' sorority, Pi Beta Alpha, and was the head of the cheerleading squad. Elizabeth, on the other hand, was a serious student with high aspirations to be a journalist. She was actively involved in extracurricular activities and wrote the "Personal Profiles" column for *The Oracle*, the school newspaper.

But despite their differences, there had always been an intangible link between the two of them. The bond the twins shared was closer than that of any siblings Elizabeth knew. They often communicated to each other through looks rather than words. And when one of them was in trouble, they seemed to read each other's thoughts. But now it seemed as if

Jessica were completely out of reach, thought Elizabeth despondently as she watched Jessica and Jeremy gaze into each other's eyes. She sighed audibly, tired of witnessing the tender reconciliation between the two lovebirds.

"So what happened next?" asked Jessica, her blue-green eyes sparkling brightly. She pulled her knees up to her chest and settled comfortably into the kitchen chair.

"I went after you when you ran off," Jeremy said. "But I couldn't find you anywhere. And when I went back to the clearing where Sue had been, she was gone."

The words seemed to reverberate in the silent kitchen and in Elizabeth's head. *She was gone, she was gone, she was gone.* Elizabeth was really worried about her friend. Sue seemed to have a flair for the dramatic when it concerned Jeremy. Elizabeth experienced a sense of déjà vu as she thought back to Sue's suicide attempt a few weeks earlier. They had all been sitting at the breakfast table together, just as they were now, when they had realized that Sue was missing. And Elizabeth had experienced a strange premonition.

She shivered as images of that fateful morning floated through her mind: Sue sprawled out on the bed, ghostly pale and barely breathing; the empty bottle of pills lying ominously on the floor; the note saying that life without Jeremy wasn't worth living; the mad rush to the hospital in the ambulance; Sue's having her stomach pumped.

And Elizabeth thought back to Sue's confession

9

that she had faked her rare blood disease in a desperate move to get Jeremy back. Elizabeth wondered what kind of extreme measures she had taken now. But then a new possibility occurred to her. What if something really *had* happened to her—a young woman alone in the woods in the middle of the night? What if she had been abducted by a band of fugitives? Or killed by a deranged murderer? Or wounded by a wild animal in the woods? Elizabeth fought down a feeling of panic.

"Well, sitting here worrying about Sue isn't helping matters," Elizabeth said, standing up suddenly. "I think we should go back to the cabin to look for her."

"But Jeremy already looked for her," Jessica protested. Elizabeth shot her sister a knowing look, fully aware that Jessica had no desire to look for Sue, let alone find her.

"It's true, I looked everywhere," agreed Jeremy, a despondent look on his face. "I turned the cabin upside down and scoured the woods around it."

Elizabeth looked from Jessica to Jeremy, both seemingly content to sit around worrying about the situation. She couldn't bear the thought of Sue alone in the woods while they sat in the comfort of the Wakefield house. They had to do something. "Well, if you two aren't coming, I'm going alone," she asserted.

Jeremy turned worried eyes to Elizabeth. "Maybe you're right," he conceded finally. "I searched the woods pretty thoroughly, but we could have better luck with three people."

"Let's go!" Elizabeth urged, grabbing her bag from the table where she had deposited it earlier.

"We don't have any time to waste." Jeremy picked up his coat and headed into the hall. Jessica sat at the table complacently with her head in her hands, watching Jeremy's receding back. "Jessica, c'mon!" Elizabeth said, taking her by the hand and yanking her up from the table.

"Ouch!" exclaimed Jessica as she knocked her ankle on the table leg.

"Shh!" cautioned Elizabeth. "We don't want to wake Mom and Dad. They'd never let us go out at this hour."

"Sorry!" Jessica returned, following her sister grudgingly into the hall. "I wouldn't make any noise if you would just let me move by myself."

Jeremy was rummaging in the hall closet. "Here," he said, handing a rain slicker to Jessica and an overcoat and hat to Elizabeth. "It's raining out."

The three of them tiptoed quietly down the hall and crept out of the house. Elizabeth turned a fearful look back into the dark hall, shutting the door quietly behind her.

Jessica took the front passenger seat of Jeremy's rented blue Ford Taurus, and Elizabeth slipped into the backseat. Jeremy carefully turned over the motor and backed down the street without turning the lights on.

Chapter 2

Elizabeth shivered as Jeremy maneuvered the car up the gravel trail leading to the Nature Cabin. The cabin, which had been so festive a few hours ago, now looked small and abandoned in the huge expanse of woods. Black and orange streamers were hanging limply from the wooden door, torn and soggy from the rain. A jack-o'-lantern smiled down at them from a road sign, grinning a macabre, crooked grin. A life-size paper skeleton was swinging back and forth from the branches of a tree.

"Well, here we are," said Jeremy, pulling the car to a stop in front of the wooden structure and jumping out. Elizabeth and Jessica followed, their feet making light crunching noises as they trod on the wet autumn leaves. Elizabeth glanced around worriedly. A full red moon dipped low in the sky, illuminating the dark, foreboding woods. She took in the eerie woods and shuddered, wondering if Sue was lost in them somewhere.

"OK," said Jeremy, spreading out a map of the area on the hood of the car. "Elizabeth, why don't you check out the stretch of woods to the west of the cabin?" He pointed in the general direction to the left of them. "And, Jessica, you can search the east woods. But don't go too far," he added. "You'll eventually meet up with the main road if you do. As for me—" Jeremy paused a moment, considering. "I'll scour the woods behind the cabin and by the riverbank."

"Jeremy, aren't you coming with me?" Jessica demanded. She obviously wasn't pleased about the idea of tromping around alone in the dark woods in the middle of the night.

"I'm afraid not, Jessica. We've got to be efficient. We don't have much time," said Jeremy, glancing at his watch worriedly.

"OK, don't worry about me," Jessica said, smiling up at Jeremy good-naturedly. Elizabeth looked over at her sister, surprised that she had given in so easily. Jessica probably didn't want Jeremy to think she was too scared to look for Sue on her own, Elizabeth surmised. She knew Jessica wanted to prove that she could be just as down-to-earth and adventuresome as Jeremy and Sue.

"Now, if we don't bump into each other sooner, let's plan to meet here by the car at three thirty," Jeremy said. "That will give us about an hour."

"We'd better get going, then," Elizabeth said,

14

turning in the direction of the west woods. "I'll see you soon."

"Elizabeth, wait a second," Jeremy said. He fished around in the glove compartment of the car and came up with a big orange flashlight. "Here, take this with you," he said, handing it to her.

Jessica looked at him expectantly. "Jess, you'll be okay with the light of the moon," Jeremy explained. "The woods are denser on the west side."

Jessica swallowed hard and forced a smile. "Sure, no problem," she bit out.

"Jess, c'mon," Elizabeth urged.

"OK, Liz," said Jessica, turning to her sister. "Let's go."

Jeremy watched as Jessica and Elizabeth made their way separately into the deep woods. As soon as they were safely out of sight, he walked quickly up to the cabin, unlocked the door, and let himself in. He picked up a lantern in the doorway and lit it with a match, holding it up to see around him. In the faint illumination of the kerosene lamp, the cabin looked like an animated Halloween scene. The walls were decorated with devilish masks and ghoulish figures, which seemed to sway and dance in the shadows of the room. Carved pumpkins lined the fireplace mantel, and purple and orange streamers adorned the walls.

Putting the lantern out, Jeremy ran lightly up the wooden staircase to the second floor. He stood for a moment in the main bedroom, allowing his eyes to adjust to the dim light. Then he searched the outlines of the ceiling until his eyes lit upon a small copper latch hidden in the wooden beams. Jeremy picked up a fishing pole from the corner and hooked it into the latch, pulling down a trapdoor. A creaky staircase slowly descended. Looking over his shoulder, he quickly climbed up the ladder leading to the attic.

"Sue! Sue!" shouted Elizabeth as she scoured the woods, shining her flashlight in front of her. It was the middle of the night on Halloween, and Elizabeth was spooked. The moon was full and the woods seemed haunted. Elizabeth looked up fearfully at the shining red orb, half expecting to see a witch on a broomstick flying past. The wind howled as it blew through the trees, whipping the branches and sending droplets of rain in Elizabeth's direction. The trees with their knotted branches looked like gnarled old men as they waved and moaned in the wind. Elizabeth turned down the rim of her cloth hat and peered through the dense thicket.

Where can Sue be? Elizabeth wondered. *Has she staged another traumatic diversion to get Jeremy back. Or what if her suicide attempt was successful this time?* Elizabeth looked up at the branch of a majestic oak tree and pictured Sue swinging lightly in the wind, hanging from the branch with a noose tied around her neck. The leaves crackled as she stepped on them, and Elizabeth looked around wildly, exhaling sharply. *Or what if some psychotic killer found her and strangled her?* worried Elizabeth. Elizabeth felt her way through the brush with caution, expecting to stumble upon the body at any moment. She shivered and wrapped her overcoat tightly around her.

"Sue, Sue!" Elizabeth called softly, shining the flashlight in the woods around her. She looked back in the direction of the cabin, wondering how Jessica and Jeremy were faring. She thought she saw a light shining from the attic. Elizabeth squinted her eyes to see more clearly, tripping over a pumpkin in the process. She regained her balance and looked down. A gaping mouth smiled up at her. Elizabeth screamed involuntarily, thinking for a moment that she had stumbled upon a head.

Get hold of yourself, Elizabeth, she told herself sternly, crouching down and wrapping her arms around her body. She glanced fearfully back at the cabin, which was now shrouded in darkness. *Now you're seeing human heads and imaginary lights.* Elizabeth took a deep breath and berated herself for her irrational fears. She couldn't let her own anxiety get in the way of her duty toward Sue. She was letting her imagination run away with her. Sue had probably just wandered away and gotten lost in the woods, and she would be fine—just as soon as they found her.

Elizabeth regained her composure, then got up and resumed her hunt. "Sue, Sue!" she cried.

What in the world am I doing here? wondered Jessica to herself for the tenth time as she looked around the deserted woods. She stepped carefully through the damp brush, unhappy to be alone in the woods in the middle of the night. She felt scared and vulnerable, with nothing—and nobody—to protect her. Suddenly a black bat flew overhead, screeching as it passed her. Jessica screamed, covering her head with her hands and diving to the ground.

A bat! Jessica thought in horror. *That's it,* she decided, standing up cautiously as she wiped clods of dirt and wet leaves off her body. She'd had enough. It was one thing to be alone in the woods in the dead of night, but quite another to contend with vampires. She would wait for Jeremy and Elizabeth in the warmth and safety of the car.

Jessica turned and headed back to the cabin but stopped after she'd gone a few feet. What would Jeremy think when he found out she had just waited in the car while he and Elizabeth had done all the work? He would think she was a coward, a spoiled prima donna who was afraid of the dark. And he would realize that she didn't care about Sue's welfare. He would think she was selfish and unfeeling. No, Jessica said to herself, she had to endure this hour, bats and all.

Jessica looked around the woods surrounding her, searching for some sort of weapon. She noticed a cracked branch hanging off a dead tree in front of her. She pulled at the limb, twisting it at the root until it ripped off the trunk. *There, a walking stick,* she thought with satisfaction, wringing her red hands. Her spirits lifted as she wandered on through the woods, feeling a little more courageous with her wooden staff to protect her.

Her thoughts turned to Jeremy as she ambled

through the woods. Thinking of him made her feel awake and alive, and her love for him seemed to fill the woodland around her.

Finally Jessica leaned back against a wet tree, pulling on the hood of her yellow slicker to shelter her from the wet bark. She was beginning to feel tired and annoyed again. Why was she risking her life for Sue, anyway? After all, Sue really was the last person in the world she'd want to find. In fact, if she would disappear for good, Jessica wouldn't have to worry about Sue's pathetic efforts to get Jeremy back.

Really, why doesn't the girl give up? thought Jessica in exasperation. She was getting fed up with Sue's attention-getting ploys. When Elizabeth had told her that Sue had been afflicted with the same rare blood disease that had killed her mother, Jessica had felt guilty for intervening in their marriage. She had felt somehow responsible for the whole thing, as if she had magically willed the disease. But then it turned out that Sue had made up the whole thing to keep Jeremy. *Just as I figured,* thought Jessica in satisfaction. *And now the conniving little witch has got us out here again, looking for her.* She sighed and resumed her lackluster search, hacking aimlessly through the woods with her walking stick.

"Jeremy!" Sue said, her voice small and frightened. "You're back!" Sue was huddled on the floor of the dark, dusky attic, her knees folded up to her chest. Her eyes looked enormous in her small face with its chin-length dark hair.

"That's right, I'm back, sweetheart," Jeremy said, kneeling down beside her and draping an arm around her.

"I thought you'd never return," Sue said, her voice plaintive. "Jeremy, please don't leave me here again. It's horrible sitting up here in the dark. It's cramped and dusty, and there are bats! They look vicious."

Sue pointed up to the far corner of the attic. A cluster of bats hung upside down from the ceiling beams. As if to illustrate her point, one of the bats opened its wings and swooped down on them. Sue opened her mouth to scream, but Jeremy grabbed her and covered her mouth. Holding her still with one hand, he picked up an old fishing rod with the other and beat the bat away.

"Sue, be quiet!" Jeremy hissed. "It's a harmless mammal. You know that." Sue looked downcast. Jeremy continued in a reprimanding tone. "We've been on hundreds of nature hikes together, and you've never been afraid of any creature—bird, reptile, rodent, or mammal."

"I know," Sue agreed, looking bashful. "But it's different being caged up here with them."

"Well, just be patient," Jeremy urged. "Remember, a few more hours and the inheritance will finally be ours. And all of our suffering will have been worth it."

"I guess you're right," Sue said, feeling unconvinced.

Jeremy picked up an old flashlight from the floor and blew on it, spreading a trail of dust in the air. He shined the flashlight on Sue for an instant, and she recoiled, blinded by the light. Suddenly he yanked the gold necklace she was wearing off her neck. "Jeremy, what are you doing?" Sue exclaimed, grabbing her hand instinctively to her bare throat.

"Trust me, sweetheart," Jeremy droned, dropping the delicate chain into his pocket.

"But, Jeremy, that's the locket my mother gave to me on my sixteenth birthday," Sue protested. "It's got her picture in it."

"Don't worry, you'll get it back," Jeremy said, standing up. "Now, I've got to go. Do you remember how to work the recorder?"

"I remember, but—" Sue began.

"Shh," said Jeremy, and leaned in to give her a warm kiss on the lips. He sat down and rubbed her back, trying not to let his impatience show. "Just sit tight, honey. And remember, I'll be back soon. Now, what time do the twins leave for school in the morning?"

"Umm, around seven thirty, I think," said Sue, biting her lip.

"Okay, then, at exactly seven fifteen tomorrow morning, we'll get this thing rolling," said Jeremy, rubbing his hands together excitedly. "Now, let's synchronize our watches. It's three o'clock by my watch."

Jeremy knelt down and shined the lantern on Sue's wrist. As she bent her head to adjust the time, she was overcome by a feeling of fear. Jeremy blew out the lantern as soon as she had finished, and she sat quietly for a moment, adjusting to the dusky moonlight. Sue looked up at the cluster of bats.

Animals never attack unless they're provoked, she reflected, thinking back to the bat's mad flight. It was a bad omen. Sue realized that she had to stop this crazy scheme before it was too late. She couldn't imagine how she had let things go this far, but she knew one thing for sure—she had to stop it now. She turned to face Jeremy, a look of determination in her dark-brown eyes.

"Jeremy—" she began, and looked around wildly. He was gone.

Elizabeth made her way back toward the cabin, her arms sore from clawing through the brush and her voice hoarse from yelling. It was almost three thirty, and she was beginning to lose faith. She hoped that Jeremy and Jessica had had better luck than she had. An owl hooted directly in front of her and she jumped. She looked up into the glowing eyes of the woodenlike bird and backed away fearfully, running smack into another person. "Aaagghh!" Elizabeth let out a bloodcurdling scream and jumped back.

"Jessica!" Elizabeth exclaimed, letting out her breath.

"Jeez, Liz, you scared me half to death!" Jessica exclaimed. "Why don't you watch where you're going?"

"Sorry," Elizabeth said. She shook her head hard, trying to calm the beating of her heart.

"Hey, did you find something?" called Jeremy, running through the woods toward them. Jessica paused to look at him, admiring his taut frame as he loped gracefully toward them. With his golden hair and gold-flecked brown eyes, he looked like a leopard bounding through the jungle. Jessica imagined him leading a dangerous expedition in a rain forest in Brazil, looking brave and powerful as he courageously fought to save the environment.

"No, we didn't find anything," said Elizabeth despondently when Jeremy reached them.

"Well, I found this," Jeremy said, his voice grim. He pulled a heart-shaped golden locket from his pocket and held up the broken chain. "It was in the driveway. Sue's mother gave it to her—before she died."

Elizabeth shivered, the words "before she died" echoing in her head. She took the locket from Jeremy and carefully opened the delicate clasp. An older version of Sue gazed up at her from the tiny frame. Elizabeth stared down at the lovely image, mesmerized by the likeness. She handed the locket back to Jeremy, a worried frown creasing her brow. "Sue would have been extra careful with this," she said.

"I know," Jeremy agreed, looking downcast. "That necklace means the world to her."

"Oh, it probably just fell off when she left the party," said Jessica, waving her hand dismissively.

"Unfortunately, I don't think so," Jeremy said, holding up the necklace and pointing out the broken chain. "The clasp is still intact."

"Do you think it came off in some sort of struggle?" Elizabeth asked hesitatingly.

"That's what I'm afraid of," said Jeremy, a look of grave concern on his face.

"You two are being so dramatic," said Jessica, scoffing. "Sue is a grown woman and can take care of herself. She is probably in bed at this very moment, sleeping like a baby—while we're standing here chatting in the drizzle."

"But, Jess, she would have been back before two A.M.," insisted Elizabeth.

"Well, then, maybe she got a ride home with someone from Project Nature and is staying with them, safe and sound," Jessica offered.

"Somehow I doubt it," said Elizabeth, shaking her head. "Sue's always so responsible. If she stayed out, I'm sure she'd call." She paused and thought for a moment. "Well, I guess it's worth checking out, anyway. Jeremy, you're friends with all the guests from Project Nature who were at the party. Why don't we go inside and call them?"

"Unfortunately, there isn't a phone in the cabin," said Jeremy. "See," he added, pointing at the unobstructed nature scene around him. "No phone lines."

"There's a cellular phone in one of the bedrooms," piped up Jessica. "Lila used it to call her mom." Lila Fowler was Jessica's best friend.

"Oh, right," said Jeremy. He hesitated a moment, thinking. "But I don't have my address book with me—it's in my room." Jeremy had rented a room for a month in a resident hotel in downtown Sweet Valley.

"Well, there goes that idea," Elizabeth said, looking downcast. "What are we going to do now?"

"Why don't I make the calls myself when I get back to my room?" Jeremy suggested.

"Well, I guess that's the best plan for now," said

Elizabeth with a sigh, taking one last look into the woods for signs of Sue.

"Definitely," agreed Jessica, thrilled to finally leave the Nature Cabin and the spooky woods. Jessica, Elizabeth, and Jeremy piled back into the car to head back to Sweet Valley. Jessica flipped on the radio as they headed onto the main road, turning the knob adeptly until she reached her favorite station. The sounds of a popular rock song blasted forth from the dashboard.

"Do you think you could turn that down?" Elizabeth asked.

"You don't like 'Purple Rain' anymore?" asked Jessica, twisting around to see her sister. Elizabeth was curled up in the backseat of the car, her eyes closed. "Oh, sorry," Jessica said, turning the sound down. She hummed softly to the music and leaned over to rest her head on Jeremy's shoulder. He didn't respond to her gesture, keeping both hands gripped tightly on the steering wheel.

"Looks like the rain has stopped," Jessica said softly, leaning back to look at Jeremy's profile. With his wavy, golden-blond hair and strong, defined features, he looked like the picture of Michelangelo's David she had seen in her art class the week before.

"Hmm," Jeremy responded, his eyes on the road.

"Maybe we can do something together tomorrow," Jessica ventured. Jeremy was silent. "Like go out to eat or see a movie."

Jessica could see Jeremy's jaw clench. "Jessica, I don't think we can go out and have fun until we find Sue," he said finally, his voice even.

Jessica wanted to scream. She was tired of hearing about Sue and worrying about Sue and looking for Sue. Jeremy had just gotten back from his business trip to Costa Rica, and all he could think of was Sue. He had been gone for over a month, and this was one of their first nights back together. Jessica opened her mouth to express her indignation at being neglected but realized she would just sound petty and jealous. She fell back in her seat, silent. Well, Jessica thought, she would just have to find some way to get Jeremy alone the next day. Then maybe she could get some of his attention too.

Elizabeth woke up with a start as Jeremy pulled up to the split-level house on Calico Drive. "Home sweet home," Jeremy said.

"It doesn't feel so sweet without Sue in it," said Elizabeth dryly. "You'll call tonight with any news, right?" she asked Jeremy as she got out of the car. "I'll pick up the phone on the first ring."

"You can count on it," said Jeremy. "But in any case, I'll come by in the morning before school to discuss the situation with your family."

"OK," said Elizabeth. "But don't mention anything about me and Jessica. My parents would kill us if they knew we were out in the woods in the middle of the night."

"My lips are sealed," Jeremy reassured her.

"See you tomorrow, then," said Elizabeth, managing a dispirited wave. She turned and headed wearily to the house.

"Good night," Jeremy returned. "And don't

worry," he called after her. "We'll find Sue if it's the last thing we do."

Jessica didn't think she could bear to hear one more word about Jeremy's whimpering, simpering, manipulative ex-fiancée. Jeremy leaned over to kiss her good night, but she jumped out of the car before he could reach her, slamming the door in a huff and storming up the walk.

Chapter 3

Elizabeth woke up early Monday morning from a fitful sleep, feeling confused. She gazed around her room, wondering why she felt so disquieted. Suddenly the events of the previous evening came flooding back to her: Jessica's emotional entrance at the party, Sue's mysterious disappearance, Jeremy's unexpected arrival, the terrifying late-night search in the woods of the Nature Cabin. Elizabeth rubbed her eyes wearily and sat up in bed. She glanced at the clock on the nightstand. It was only six thirty. A beam of sunlight was shining through her bedroom window, creating a bright shaft of sparkling dust particles. Elizabeth felt calmer in the light of the early morning. Maybe they were all just spooked because it was Halloween, she told herself hopefully. Maybe Jessica was right—maybe Sue just stayed with some friends last night. Or maybe she went out

29

after the party and got a ride home later. Maybe, maybe, maybe . . .

Elizabeth hopped out of bed and slipped into a light cotton robe. She made her way quietly out of the bedroom, hoping against hope that Sue had come back and was sleeping soundly in her bed in Steven's bedroom. But as she padded across the hall in her bare feet to her brother's room, she realized with a sinking feeling that Sue hadn't come back. The eerie premonition she had experienced the night before returned to her now in full force.

Elizabeth knocked lightly on the door. There was no response. She took a deep breath and slowly pushed it open, picturing Sue lying perfectly still on the bed, an empty pill bottle by her side. The door swung open, revealing a vacant room. The small room was in impeccable order, and the bed was made up perfectly, the way Sue left it yesterday morning and every morning. The bed looked cold and sterile, as if it belonged in a hospital. Elizabeth fought back the urge to rumple the covers and shake out the feeling of death the neatly made-up bed evoked.

She sighed, realizing that she had to tell her parents. She thought back to all they'd been through lately, from Jessica's breaking up Sue and Jeremy's wedding to her declaration that she and Jeremy were engaged. Elizabeth couldn't stand the idea of putting her parents through anything else.

As she paused by the banister for a moment, she thought over the events of the last few weeks. Jessica's intervention at Sue and Jeremy's wedding had sent her parents over the edge. They had threatened to send her to Milford Academy for Girls, a boarding school in Washington State. But Sue, of all people, had intervened on Jessica's behalf. Maybe boarding school really was the best option for Jessica at this point, Elizabeth reflected. Even though Jessica was planning to wait for two years, Elizabeth couldn't bear the thought of her sister getting married at the age of eighteen and throwing away her future.

Elizabeth forced the thought of Jessica's engagement from her mind. That problem would have to wait until later. Right now the most important thing was to find Sue. And the next order of business was to let her parents know Sue was missing. Elizabeth headed purposefully down the hall to her parents' bedroom.

Jessica stood alone in the center of the ghostly Halloween ball. The dance floor was crowded with ghoulish figures dancing spookily together. Witches and warlocks were waltzing across the floor, and devils and demons were tangoing together. The woods were animated and illuminated by a large, glowing red ball. A bony white skeleton and an ugly black witch were dancing a solo dance by the moonlight. They slowly transformed into Jeremy and Sue, who were locked in an intimate embrace, their kiss highlighted by the moonlight. The setting faded into an altar, and Jeremy and Sue were kissing after having taken their vows. Suddenly the moment was freeze-framed and was being replayed on a video at Sweet Valley High. The kids in the classroom hooted and cheered, clapping wildly for the perfect couple. The camera zoomed in to a close-up of their lips, which transformed into a pair of huge red clown lips with enormous white teeth, filling the screen. The mouth was wide-open and laughing—laughing, laughing, laughing—HA HA HA HA HA!!!

Jessica bolted up in bed, her body drenched in sweat. She breathed a sigh of relief as she realized that she'd been dreaming. She leaned back against the wall, the images replaying in her head. She had forgotten all about the disturbing video she had recently seen of a couple kissing, a couple who bore a striking resemblance to Jeremy and Sue. Her friend Amy Sutton had joined a video club, and Jessica had gone to a meeting where they had screened the student films. One of the videos had featured Sweet Valley's hottest kissing spots, and one of the shots in the video had presented a strangely familiar couple kissing on a deserted beach on a cloudy, misty day. Jessica reassured herself again that it was only her imagination running away with her, inserting Jeremy and Sue into the screen. She shook her head hard, trying to banish the troubling images from her mind.

Voices from downstairs wafted up the steps. Jessica heard her parents talking with Elizabeth in the kitchen and remembered everything—Jeremy's explanation of the night before and Sue's disappearance. *What a night,* Jessica thought to herself, realizing why she felt so tired. She hoped Sue had safely returned to the house so she would stop commanding everybody's attention. Jessica listened closely, but judging by the animated tone in her parents' frantic voices, Sue had clearly not been found.

Jessica wrapped her comforter tightly around her, still feeling the impact of the dream. If only she could spend some time with Jeremy alone, she knew she'd feel better. In the calm of the morning Jessica regretted her impetuous departure of the night before. She was anxious to restore good feelings between herself and Jeremy. She looked at her clock on the bedside table—it was a little before seven o'clock. Jeremy would be there any minute. Jessica kicked back the covers and jumped out of bed, hoping to intercept him before he came to the door. Then they could be alone for a few moments before her parents descended on him.

Jessica ran into the bathroom and splashed cold water on her face. She dressed quickly, pulling on a pair of tight black jeans and a mint-green scoop-neck T-shirt. A thick brown leather belt completed the effect—casual, but sexy. Jessica touched up her lips with strawberry lip gloss and quickly ran a brush through her golden-blond hair. She bent over, flipping her hair foward, then straightened, her hair settling in fluffy waves around her shoulders. Jessica smiled into the mirror, pleased with her reflection. *Not bad for three hours' sleep,* she told herself. When Jeremy saw her today, all thoughts of Sue would vanish from his mind.

Jessica skipped out of the room, excited at the thought of spending some time with Jeremy alone. But as she was making her way down the hall, she heard the doorbell ring. She stopped as she was half-way down the steps and watched with dismay as Mr. Wakefield flung open the door, greeting a haggard-looking Jeremy.

". . . so I scoured the entire woods, but there was no trace of her," finished Jeremy, a weary expression on his face.

The Wakefields and Jeremy were settled in the living room. Mr. and Mrs. Wakefield sat on the sofa with Elizabeth between them, and Jeremy sat in the armchair across from them. A pot of cold coffee sat untouched on a trivet plate in the middle of the marble coffee table. Jessica was sitting cross-legged on the rug, a dour expression on her face. She listened dully to the conversation as she slowly brought spoonfuls of blueberry yogurt to her mouth.

"That means she's been missing for over five hours," said Ned Wakefield, a look of concern on his face.

"That's right," said Jeremy, nodding solemnly. "I came by late last night, hoping to find her here, but Jessica and Elizabeth were the only ones here." He shrugged his shoulders and spread out his hands in a wide gesture.

"Why didn't you wake us when Jeremy came over?" Mr. Wakefield asked, turning to Elizabeth.

Jessica noticed her sister swallow hard. She wondered how Elizabeth would answer the question. The girls didn't want their parents to know that they too had been searching for Sue in the middle of the night. Mr. and Mrs. Wakefield would be furious if they found out that they had undertaken such a dangerous task by themselves. "Uhh, we didn't want to jump to conclusions," Elizabeth stammered finally. "We thought that maybe Sue had decided to stay with a friend." *Nice going, sis,* thought Jessica with a smile.

"That's a possibility," said Alice Wakefield, her eyes lighting up with hope.

"Not anymore," said Jeremy, his tone weary. "I called everybody from Project Nature last night, and nobody has any idea of her whereabouts."

"Ned, we've got to do something right away," urged Alice, her voice panicked. "Sue is like a daughter to me." Jessica groaned inwardly at her mother's words. First Sue had tried to steal her fiancé, and now she was stealing her mother.

Ned Wakefield took his wife's hand. "I'll arrange for a search party immediately," he said. "Those woods are sprawling. Anybody could easily get lost in them."

"Ned, I think we should call the police. With the weather the way it was last night, Sue could have had a serious accident," put in Mrs. Wakefield. "Maybe she fell and broke her leg, or worse. . . ." Her voice trailed off.

"You're right, Alice," agreed Ned. "Anything's possible. I'm going to call the police." Mr. Wakefield stood up and reached for the phone.

"Wait!" Jeremy cried, anxiously looking at his watch.

All eyes turned to Jeremy expectantly. "Uh, maybe Sue's with Robby," said Jeremy, referring to his friend, Robby Goodman. Robby was dating Lila

Fowler and was friends with Sue as well. "I couldn't get hold of him last night. And he's probably up by now." Jeremy glanced at the brass clock on the mantel. The clock read 7:14.

"Why don't you give him a call?" suggested Mrs. Wakefield.

"Uh, yeah, good idea," said Jeremy, his eyes still following the hands of the clock.

Ned put his hand on the phone, ready to give it to Jeremy, when it jangled in his hand. Ned jumped involuntarily, then picked up the receiver. "Yes?" he asked. His face creased into a frown, and he held up his hand to the others to signal quiet. The room was perfectly still as he put the call on the speakerphone.

Everybody sat in silence as a muffled tone came across the line.

"You don't know me, but I know you," said an ominous male voice. "I've got Sue. But don't worry, she's safe and sound." Jessica frowned, feeling the voice was vaguely familiar. She tried to place it, wondering who would have abducted Sue. For the first time since Sue had disappeared, Jessica felt worried. Sue really was in danger. "That, that voice—" she began.

"Jessica, quiet!" Elizabeth said, leaning in closer to hear. Elizabeth was stunned. Sue had been kidnapped! They hadn't even considered that. A tremor of fear passed through her body as the menacing voice continued.

"And I would be happy to give her back to you," said the gravelly voice, speaking slowly, "for the small sum of five hundred thousand dollars."

Half a million dollars! The exact amount of Sue's inheritance! Elizabeth's eyes widened, and she and Jessica exchanged glances. Elizabeth's mind ticked away as she struggled to make sense of the information. Sue's mother had stipulated in her will that Sue's inheritance would default to Alice Wakefield if Sue remained with Jeremy, of whom she disapproved. But if Sue was not with him for a period of two months, the money would legally belong to Sue. And today, November 1, was the day Sue was to receive the money. So somebody must have known about it. And somehow known that it would go to Sue today, unless—unless someone else got his hands on it first. Elizabeth's mind whirled, trying to make sense of it. Who else had known about the money?

"And one last thing," continued the voice. "If you call the police, don't expect to see Sue again." The voice paused and static filled the line. "At least, not alive." A chill traveled slowly down Elizabeth's spine.

"But don't do anything yet," finished the voice ominously. "I'll keep in touch. Expect me at five o'clock tonight. Sharp." The phone went dead.

A stunned silence followed the call; then everybody started speaking at once.

"I can't believe it! Sue's been kidnapped!" Elizabeth said, standing up suddenly.

"Half a million dollars!" exclaimed Jessica.

"Do you think she's OK?" asked Elizabeth worriedly, turning to face her parents.

"Yeah, what if they've already killed her?" surmised Jessica.

37

"Jessica! Don't even think something like that!" reprimanded Elizabeth.

"The poor girl!" said Mrs. Wakefield. "She must be scared out of her mind."

"So am I," said Elizabeth, fighting back tears as she thought about her friend. Elizabeth had been kidnapped before, and she knew what it was like. When she had worked as a volunteer at Sweet Valley's hospital, Carl, an orderly, had fallen in love with her—so much so that he had abducted her and taken her to an isolated shack, planning to keep her with him forever. Fortunately, her friends and family had saved her. Elizabeth wondered if they could do the same for Sue now. Mrs. Wakefield pulled Elizabeth toward her and put comforting arms around her.

"OK, everybody, quiet down," said Ned, raising his voice over the others. "If we want to help Sue, we've got to stay calm." He waited a few moments until everybody settled down. "Now, the first order of business is to figure out who would do such a thing. Jeremy, does Sue have any enemies?"

Jeremy shook his head. "None that I know of," he said.

"Of course she doesn't!" interjected Alice. "Sue's so sweet, she couldn't be anybody's enemy." Jessica rolled her eyes at her mother's words. Her parents had no idea how calculating and manipulative Sue was. They didn't know anything about Sue's faked terminal illness; Sue had asked Jessica and Elizabeth not to tell them about it.

"Well, I think it's clear that the kidnapper's motive

isn't Sue, but her fortune," said Mr. Wakefield.

"But who else knows about the money?" wondered Elizabeth aloud.

"Let's see," reflected Mrs. Wakefield. "I don't think Sue has many close relatives. In fact, the only other person in her family who would have been involved at all is her stepfather, Phil."

"I bet Phil's behind all this," declared Jessica. "He has an evil face. He probably planned it all at the wedding."

"Jessica, that's pure conjecture," protested Elizabeth. "Phil was very nice, and Sue was thrilled he was here."

"OK, girls," said Ned, holding up a hand. "This isn't getting us anywhere. We're not professional sleuths. I'm afraid we're going to have to call the police despite the kidnapper's threat."

"But—but you can't do that!" Jeremy sputtered, objecting vehemently. "Didn't you hear what the kidnapper said? He's going to kill Sue if you call the police."

"I will not be threatened by some thug," asserted Ned.

"Dad!" objected Jessica. "Jeremy is not a thug!"

"Jessica!" Ned said, exasperated. "I was talking about the kidnapper, not about Jeremy."

"Oh," said Jessica demurely, and fell silent. Elizabeth watched the exchange with interest. Even though they wouldn't express it, she knew her parents disapproved of Jeremy just as much as she did. They respected his environmental work, but they didn't appreciate the fact that he had cheated on his fiancée, nor that he had gotten engaged to their sixteen-year-old daughter.

"Ned, perhaps Jeremy's right," interjected Mrs. Wakefield. "Sue's in serious danger. We can't risk jeopardizing her life."

"Yeah," agreed Jeremy, an impassioned look on his face. "The most important thing is Sue's life, not the money."

Jessica pondered that for a moment. If Sue was gone, not only would she have Jeremy, but the money as well. Mrs. Wakefield would probably put the money in a trust fund for her daughters, and then Jessica and Elizabeth would each come into a quarter of a million dollars when they turned twenty-one. Jessica envisioned herself at twenty-one, a famous actress with a renowned husband. She and Jeremy would buy a huge house on the Malibu coast with a private yacht. They would throw wild parties and mix with all the Hollywood stars.

Elizabeth watched as Jessica's eyes took on a familiar faraway look. She was well aware that Jessica regretted having to make a choice between her love of money and her love for Jeremy. And she was sure that Jessica was busy spending her fortune now. Elizabeth caught Jessica's eye and sent her a dirty look. Jessica returned her look with an innocent, wide-eyed stare. Elizabeth turned away. If anything happened to Sue, she resolved, she would donate her share of the fortune to wildlife. A tear welled in her eye at the thought.

Now Ned was pacing back and forth. "Yes, the most important thing is Sue's life," he agreed. "But we can't just play by their rules and leave Sue in their hands."

Suddenly Mrs. Wakefield's eyes lit up. "Ned, what about that special detective you know in L.A., your old college buddy, Sam Diamond—the one who solved that jewelry theft last year? Remember—the case where the woman faked the theft of her own jewels in order to claim the insurance money?"

Ned snapped his fingers. "That's it!" he exclaimed. "Yes, Sam would be perfect."

Elizabeth noticed Jeremy shift uncomfortably in his seat at Mrs. Wakefield's words. "We can't call a detective," Jeremy protested, his voice rising in frustration. "If we involve an outside party, we'll be putting Sue in grave danger." Purple veins popped out on his neck as he spoke.

"Jeremy," said Mr. Wakefield firmly, "I'm afraid she's already in grave danger as it is."

"B-but—" Jeremy objected.

Mr. Wakefield held up a firm hand. "I think this is a good compromise. The kidnapper said not to call the police. And we're not calling the police. We're contacting a detective."

Jeremy nodded and stared at the ground.

Mr. Wakefield went to the study and returned with his address book. He flipped through the pages until he got to the number, then picked up the phone and dialed. "Hello, Sam, it's Ned, Ned Wakefield. . . . It's been a while, I know. . . . Listen, I've got a rather peculiar case here. . . ."

41

Chapter 4

"Well, there's nothing else we can do right now, so we might as well have breakfast," Mrs. Wakefield said, ushering everybody out of the room. Elizabeth grabbed the coffeepot off the table and followed her mother into the hall.

"C'mon, sweetie," Jessica said, getting up and holding out a hand to Jeremy. He took her outstretched hand and followed along distractedly as she led him out of the room. Jessica stopped in the dining room and looked him in the eyes, wanting desperately to reestablish contact with him. Jeremy looked back at her blankly, a faraway expression on his face.

"Jeremy," Jessica began softly, "I'm sorry about last night."

Jeremy gave her a vacant stare. "About last night?" he asked.

"About my, uh, abrupt departure. I didn't kiss you good night," Jessica explained. She looked deep into his midnight-brown eyes, but the expression in them was unfathomable.

"Oh, that . . ." Jeremy said, waving a hand dismissively.

"Well, I'd like to make up for it now," Jessica said in a soft, sultry voice. She was tired of his neglect, and she knew one foolproof way to get his attention. She leaned toward him and pressed her mouth against his. He was resistant at first, but then he slowly began to warm up, responding with more and more passion until he was kissing her with an urgency that made her dizzy.

"Mom, how can you think of food at a time like this?" Elizabeth asked, accompanying her mother to the kitchen.

"Frankly, Liz, I don't think any of us have much of an appetite. But we've got to keep up our strength, for Sue's sake," said Mrs. Wakefield.

"That's true," conceded Elizabeth, opening the refrigerator and taking out a carton of milk and a handful of eggs. "How about my famous blueberry pancakes?"

"Perfect," said Mrs. Wakefield, turning to Elizabeth with a grateful smile. "Jessica! Jeremy!" she called.

"Coming, Mom!" Jessica returned, her voice muffled.

Mrs. Wakefield gave Elizabeth an unexpected hug and turned to set the table. Elizabeth watched her mother with concern as she began mixing ingredients together in a wooden bowl. She knew Mrs. Wakefield felt responsible for Sue. And she knew she was also worried about her daughters. After all, if the kidnapper would abduct Sue for the money entrusted to Alice Wakefield, why wouldn't he go after the twins as well? Elizabeth shivered at the thought. She threw the pancake batter with unexpected force into a frying pan, watching as it sizzled loudly, a rivulet of steam rising into the air.

"Pancakes!" Jessica exclaimed with surprise, sniffing as she came into the room with Jeremy. "But we're going to be late for school," she said, looking at her watch.

"Girls, I'm afraid there will be no school for either of you until all of this is over," Alice said, scattering place mats around the butcher-block table. "I don't want you leaving the house until Sue is out of danger and her kidnapper is apprehended."

Jessica let out a whoop of delight. "Pancakes it is!" she exclaimed with joy. Elizabeth sent her a withering look. How could Jessica be so light at a time like this?

"I'm afraid I won't be able to join you," said Jeremy, his large frame hunched against the refrigerator. "I've got some urgent work to do for the Costa Rican assignment concerning the rain forests." Elizabeth looked at Jeremy in surprise. How could his work be so pressing that it took precedence over his concern for Sue? She studied his face for an answer, but his expression was inscrutable.

"Jeremy, can't it wait?" Jessica pleaded. "After all, we all need to stick together to help Sue." *Interesting how Jessica has developed a sudden concern for Sue,* thought Elizabeth to herself wryly.

"Unfortunately, it can't," Jeremy said, his voice full of regret. "I'm expecting a conference call at nine o'clock from the head of the Costa Rican Environmental Agency. If I'm not at the hotel to take this call, the whole deal could fall through. And we could lose thousands of acres of trees."

Jessica looked downcast. "Don't worry," Jeremy said, chucking her chin. "I'll come back in a few hours, just as soon as I've taken care of this call." Jessica's eyes lit up and she smiled at him. She wrapped her arm around his waist and began walking with him to the door.

Elizabeth watched them leave together, annoyed by Jessica's show of devotion to Jeremy. What was happening to her sister? What had happened to the spirited, headstrong Jessica she used to know?

"Umm, looks good," said Jessica, taking in the breakfast spread appreciatively. Everybody was seated around the kitchen table, a warm batch of fresh blueberry pancakes set out on a platter in front of them. As Jessica began to maneuver a tall stack of pancakes onto her plate, a car horn blared from the driveway.

"Now, who would that be?" asked Mrs. Wakefield.

Elizabeth jumped up, alarmed. "What if it's the kidnappers?"

"Maybe it's a rescue squad," suggested Jessica, placing the steaming pancakes onto her plate and jumping up.

"OK, everybody, stay calm," Mrs. Wakefield said,

the fear in her eyes belying her even tone. "Girls, stay here."

But Jessica was already racing into the living room. She pulled back the heavy damask curtains and peeked out the window, recognizing Lila's lime-green Triumph parked in the driveway. She tried to catch her friend's attention, but Lila was busy looking in the mirror, a stick of crimson lipstick in her hand. Jessica tapped softly on the windowpane. Finally Lila looked up and waved.

"Just a minute!" Jessica mouthed, holding up her right index finger. "It's Lila," Jessica reported as she returned to the kitchen. "She said she'd drive me to school today because Elizabeth has an *Oracle* powwow."

"Oh, that's right!" said Elizabeth. She had forgotten all about the meeting scheduled for this morning. The *Oracle* staff had planned to go over the layout for the upcoming exclusive fall sports issue. Well, the staff would just have to get by without her on this one, thought Elizabeth.

Two short blasts sounded from Lila's car. "Looks like Her Majesty is losing patience," remarked Elizabeth wryly. Even though she didn't usually express it, Elizabeth thought rich Lila Fowler was one of the most pretentious and self-centered girls in school.

"I'll be right back," said Jessica, jumping up and turning to the door, but this time Mrs. Wakefield reached out an arm and stopped her.

"Jessica," she said, her voice grave, "you can't give Lila any information whatsoever about why you're

47

missing school. If anybody finds out about the kidnapping, it could endanger Sue's life."

"Of course not!" Jessica said, her voice indignant. "I'll just tell Lila I'm sick."

Now the doorbell rang. "On second thought," said Mrs. Wakefield, getting up, "I'll take care of it myself." She gave Jessica an "I mean business" look and walked toward the door. Elizabeth tried not to smile. Jessica was infamous for her inability to keep a secret.

"Hrrmph!" said Jessica, slumping down in her seat.

Lila could see the outlines of Alice Wakefield's face glancing out the living-room window. She waited impatiently while Mrs. Wakefield opened the door hesitantly, looking around her as if she expected to encounter alien creatures. Her face looked wan and drawn, as if she hadn't slept in weeks.

"Hi, Lila," said Mrs. Wakefield, forcing a friendly smile.

"Uh, hi," answered Lila, wondering why Mrs. Wakefield was acting so bizarre. "I suppose Jessica's still getting dressed." *Putting on her makeup is more like it,* she thought. Sighing, she shifted her weight from one foot to the other. Sometimes Jessica primped and preened in the morning as if she had a debutante ball ahead of her, not a normal day of school.

"Actually, Jessica's not feeling well. She won't be in school today," said Mrs. Wakefield quickly. She looked surreptitiously over her shoulder down the hall.

"Oh, what's wrong?" asked Lila, following her gaze. "Does she have the flu?" Lila had seen Jessica run out of the party the night before, a flustered Elizabeth fast in tow. Maybe she had gotten violently ill at the party. She *had* been drinking a lot of apple cider. Not to mention the numerous caramel-covered apples she had consumed.

"Uh, yes, yes," said Mrs. Wakefield, closing the door to just a crack and fitting her body into the slot. "I think she's probably got one of those twenty-four-hour bugs."

Lila looked at Mrs. Wakefield strangely. Alice Wakefield was usually so warm and bustling, and now she was acting as if she had committed a major crime. *Any other time she would have invited me in for breakfast,* thought Lila as she became aware of the fresh aroma of buttery pancakes wafting out the door.

"Well, thanks for stopping by, dear," said Mrs. Wakefield, closing the door gently in her face. "I'll tell Jessica that you send your regards—just as soon as she wakes up."

"Uh, thanks," said Lila as the door clicked shut. Lila stared at the closed door for a moment, pondering Mrs. Wakefield's odd behavior. *As soon as she wakes up,* Mrs. Wakefield had said. But hadn't Lila just seen Jessica a few minutes ago? Was Mrs. Wakefield *lying* about Jessica's being in bed? Or had Jessica sneaked down the stairs when she wasn't looking? But, then, why had she signaled that she would be out?

Maybe Mrs. Wakefield has lost her marbles, decided Lila. *Maybe all this stuff with Jessica and*

Jeremy has finally gotten to her. She shook her head as she walked down the driveway back to her car.

"Sam's coming from Los Angeles immediately," said Ned Wakefield, walking into the kitchen. He pulled out a chair and sat down at the table next to his wife.

"Oh, Ned, this is just getting to be too much," said Alice, her eyes clouding with tears.

Mr. Wakefield put a comforting arm around her shoulders. "Don't worry," he reassured her. "Sam Diamond's the best they've got. With Sam on the trail of Sue's abductors, this case will be solved in no time."

"I'm just so worried about Sue," lamented Mrs. Wakefield. "The poor girl has been through so much."

Jessica looked down at the table. She knew her parents considered her the source of all Sue's suffering. *It isn't fair,* thought Jessica, her eyes blazing with indignation. It wasn't her fault that Jeremy had fallen in love with her before his wedding. And it certainly wasn't her fault that Sue had been kidnapped.

"Dad, would you like some pancakes?" asked Elizabeth brightly, passing the platter to her father. "I made your favorite recipe." *Perfect Elizabeth,* thought Jessica with hostility, *always lending a helping hand—while her evil twin sister ruins everything.* She knew that she was being unfair. Elizabeth was only trying to help her out, to cut some of the tension in the room. But, still, it was hard not to resent her sister's impeccable behavior.

"Thanks, Liz," said Mr. Wakefield, smiling at his daughter as he scooped a stack of pancakes onto his plate. Mrs. Wakefield picked up a pitcher of freshly squeezed orange juice and filled everybody's glasses.

"Now, Alice," said Mr. Wakefield, his voice optimistic, "don't give up hope. Remember when Elizabeth was kidnapped? We were all so worried, and it all turned out fine in the end."

"That was so awful," said Mrs. Wakefield, squeezing Elizabeth's hand. "Thank goodness we finally found you—before that lunatic took you away with him."

Elizabeth shuddered as she relived the traumatic experience. Carl had locked her up in a horrible abandoned shack, threatening to take her away with him to the mountains forever. She had spent two days tied to a hard wooden chair, with no contact with the outside world and no chance of escape. She remembered how scared and lonely and vulnerable she had felt. "But Carl wouldn't have hurt me," ventured Elizabeth. "He was in love with me. Somehow I don't think Sue is as lucky as I was."

Jessica didn't think she could stand one more moment of this conversation. If she heard one more word about poor Sue's suffering, she was going to scream. She had to speak to Jeremy, her only ally through all of this. She scraped back her chair and stood up abruptly. "May I please be excused?" she asked in a tight voice.

Jessica ran into her room and flopped down on the unmade bed, grabbing the phone receiver like a

51

lifesaver. She hesitated a moment before dialing, looking at her watch. It was just after nine o'clock. Jeremy would probably still be on his conference call. Well, she decided, she would just interrupt him for a minute and he could call her back. She quickly dialed the number of the room. No answer. She hung up and redialed, thinking that she had dialed the wrong number. Jessica lay flat on her back, her feet propped up on some throw pillows, as she listened to the phone ring over and over again. One, two, three . . . Jessica counted until the phone had rung ten times. She slammed down the receiver. *Why isn't he in his room?* she wondered. He had said he was expecting a conference call at nine A.M., an *urgent* conference call. *Where is he?* thought Jessica in frustration.

Chapter 5

"Hey, Enid, have you seen Liz around?" asked Todd Wilkins, glad to find Elizabeth's best friend, Enid Rollins, at the *Oracle* office. He hadn't seen Elizabeth in study hall that morning and had hoped to catch her at the newspaper office between classes.

"Actually, Todd, I was looking for her myself," responded Enid, a puzzled expression on her face. "I haven't seen her all day."

Todd glanced around the busy office, hoping to find Elizabeth at her usual spot, writing her "Personal Profiles" column. It was Monday morning, and the *Oracle* office was hopping. The sounds of clacking keyboards and chattering voices filled the air. Olivia Davidson was staring at a proof, meticulously reading the fine print of a feature article. Cheryl Thomas was sitting cross-legged on the floor, a full-page spread laid out in front of her. Tina Ayala, the staff photographer, was sorting through photos for the upcoming special fall sports edition. Andy Jenkins and Rod Sullivan were throwing around ideas for a sports feature and lobbing a football back and forth in the process.

"I've got it! We could cover the girls' soccer try-outs," Andy exclaimed, a mischievous glint in his deep-brown eyes. He threw the ball in the air and caught it behind his back.

"Perfect!" breathed Rod. "A behind-the-scenes look . . ."

"Nah, they'd never let us," decided Andy. "How about a swimming special—all water sports?" he suggested, tossing the ball to Rod.

"I don't know. Sounds kind of drippy to me," retorted Rod, returning the ball.

Andy groaned and whizzed the ball back. Todd intercepted it in midstream. "Hey, Jenkins, you seen Liz around?" he asked, lobbing the ball back to the muscular boy.

"No, man, sorry, can't say I have," said Andy, swiping the ball out of the air with his left hand. He cocked the ball behind his ear and faded back into the corner of the room. "Joe Montana takes the snap, steps back into the pocket, pumps right, pumps left—and lets loose with a bomb to the end zone," intoned Andy, hurling the ball across the room. "Touchdown!"

"I think 'fumble' is more like it!" said Cheryl Thomas, laughing as the ball landed in the middle of her layout and bounced under a nearby desk. Rod retrieved it quickly and tossed it back to Andy.

"Hey, hey!" said Penny Ayala, walking into the

door. Penny was the editor in chief of *The Oracle* and a good friend of Elizabeth's. "You two are supposed to report on sports here, not play them."

Andy and Rod stared at her in mock astonishment. "You mean this isn't the football stadium?" Andy asked, knocking the side of his head with his hand. "Hey, Sullivan, we've been at the wrong place the whole time."

Rod shook his head in wonder. "No wonder we couldn't find a typewriter out on the field this morning."

"Would you two get out of here!" said Penny, swiping at Andy and trying not to crack a smile.

"Aye, aye, chief!" saluted Andy.

"Hey, Penny," Todd interrupted, "has Liz been in here today?"

Penny shook her head. "No, Todd, I haven't seen her," said Penny. "Actually," she said thoughtfully, "she missed our staff meeting this morning and she didn't call in."

"That's not like Liz," said Todd, a perplexed look on his face.

"I think you're looking for Liz in all the wrong places," put in Andy with a grin. He burst out in song as he walked out of the room. "Lookin' for Liz in all the wrong places, looking for Liz in too many faces . . ."

"Lookin' for Liz," crooned Rod along with him, "when you're lookin' for Liz . . ."

"When those two clowns come into the office, this place descends into chaos," said Cheryl after the boys left the office.

"I know," said Penny, shaking her head. "Maybe

we should institute a Go *Oracle* program," she said, referring to the Go Math experiment that had taken place at Sweet Valley High a few weeks earlier. The school had taken part in a nationwide educational experiment of girls-only math classes to see if girls succeeded better in an all-girls environment.

Todd turned to Enid and spoke in a low voice. "Enid, do you think something happened after last night's incident at the Halloween party?"

Enid looked puzzled. "What incident?" she asked.

Todd pulled Enid to a deserted corner of the office. He knew she could be trusted, but he wasn't so sure about the newspaper staff. "Elizabeth had to leave the party early to take Jessica home," Todd said.

"I know. I saw them leave in a rush. I was wondering what the problem was," Enid said.

"The problem was that Jessica caught Jeremy with Sue," Todd confided. "*Making out* with Sue."

Enid's eyes opened wide. "You're kidding!" she breathed. "What a jerk!" She shook her head. "That guy is bad news. He can't be trusted with anyone. To tell you the truth, I don't know what either of them see in him."

"I don't either," agreed Todd. "He's a swine."

"Well, maybe Jessica was too upset to come to school and Elizabeth is home consoling her," suggested Enid.

"Maybe," said Todd, his voice doubtful. He swung his backpack over his right shoulder. "Well, I'd better get to class."

"I'll come with you, Todd," said Enid, pushing back her chair.

56

"What luck!" whispered Caroline Pearce to herself. She was hunched quietly behind a computer near Enid and Todd, greedily soaking in the juicy morsel of information that Todd had unwittingly unleashed. The pale, red-haired girl had a notorious reputation as the class gossip. She had come into the *Oracle* office to type an English essay before class but had stopped immediately as the scent of some hot gossip wafted by her nose. She resumed her typing as she saw Todd and Enid leave the room. *Maybe I should work here more often,* she said to herself with a wicked grin.

"I cannot believe that Bruce Patman won the costume contest last night," said Lila at lunch in the cafeteria. She dug into her chicken cutlet with a vengeance.

"I know," said Amy Sutton, her slate-gray eyes flashing. "The last thing that guy needs is a boost to his ego."

"It *is* unbelievable," chimed in Cheryl Thomas. "I mean, a Porsche, of all things." The wealthiest and best-looking guy in school, Bruce Patman, drove a sleek black Porsche with 1BRUCE1 license plates. He had been wearing a black mask at the party, but his Porsche costume was a dead giveaway.

"Well, you gotta give him credit for originality," said Ken Matthews, taking a long draw on his lemonade.

"I'll give him credit for conceit," said Lila, tossing her long brown hair over her shoulders.

"See, Maria," Winston said, "I told you that our *Star Trek* costumes weren't original enough."

Winston had come to the party bedecked as Captain Jean-Luc Picard of *Star Trek,* and Maria had accompanied him as a Vulcan with plastic pointy ears.

"Winston wanted to go to the party disguised as a pair of dice," Maria confided to the group surrounding them.

"Well, I would have preferred to be a pair of matching toothbrushes," said Winston with a goofy grin. He took a big bite of his hamburger.

"I can see you as a long-necked yellow Reach toothbrush," said Amy to Winston.

"And, Maria, you'd make a lovely pink Goody," added Ken with a grin.

"Hey, watch what you say about my woman!" said Winston, wrapping a protective arm around his girlfriend.

"There's no doubt about it, my Mona Lisa costume should have won," sulked Lila, pursing her lips together in a pout. Robby had fashioned a magnificent olive-green medieval gown for Lila. She had worn her hair in rippling waves parted down the middle to achieve the full effect.

"Li, you did look like you stepped right out of a painting," Amy said consolingly.

"Robby thought so too," said Maria with a smile. "He went around all night saying you were 'his Mona Lila.'" Lila's face brightened at her friends' comments.

"I have to admit, your costume was priceless," put in Winston, drawing a general laugh from the table.

"And you do have a very mysterious smile," added Ken.

"Thanks, Ken," said Lila, putting on a small, enigmatic grin just like that of the Mona Lisa.

"Not bad, Fowler," said Ken. "You ever think of taking up residence in the Louvre?"

"Hey, what's up, guys?" said Caroline Pearce, arriving at the table. She set down her lunch tray and squeezed onto the bench between Amy and Lila.

"Oh, hi, Caroline," Lila said, shifting in her seat to make room for her. Lila wondered what the latest scandal was, giving Caroline a suspicious look. She obviously had some juicy news to impart, or she wouldn't have insisted on taking center stage at the lunch table.

"So what were you talking about?" asked Caroline eagerly, shoveling a handful of fries into her mouth.

"Oh, we were just talking about the costumes at the Halloween party last night," said Cheryl.

"Can you believe Bruce Patman?" asked Caroline. "I mean, he came as his *car*!"

"I actually thought Jessica and Jeremy had a shot at the prize," said Cheryl. "Her Princess Jasmine costume was exquisite." Jessica had worn a pale-green harem outfit trimmed with gold, complete with a gold hair band and tiny green slippers. Jeremy had picked up the costume in L.A. on his way back from Costa Rica.

"And Jeremy made quite a striking Aladdin," put in Maria.

"I say, Maria, what are you saying?" boomed Winston in the rich British baritone of Captain Jean-Luc Picard from *Star Trek*. "Don't tell me you prefer men with more hair!" A series of disastrous haircuts had reduced Winston's full head of hair to less than a crew cut.

"No, Win, I love you just the way you are," said Maria, running a hand fondly over his stubble.

"Winston, you're a lucky man," said Ken. "Not a hairy one, but a lucky one."

Suddenly Winston looked around the table. "Where is Princess Jessica, by the way?" he asked.

"I've been wondering that myself," said Lila. "I haven't seen her all day."

"Hmm, that's interesting," said Caroline, lowering her voice. All eyes turned to her. When Caroline spoke in her slow, hushed voice, it was clear she had something of interest to impart. "Maybe she's too heartbroken to get out of bed."

Lila's ears perked up. "What do you mean—heartbroken?"

Caroline lowered her voice to a whisper, and everybody leaned in to hear. "Well, I found out that Jessica caught lover boy in the arms of another woman."

"What?" Lila exclaimed, a fierce expression crossing her even features. "Who?"

"We-ll," said Caroline, speaking in a tantalizingly slow voice. "I believe it was—Sue."

"I don't believe it," declared Lila, crossing her arms in front of her. "That's just a vicious rumor."

"Well, I happened to hear it from a *very* reliable source," insisted Caroline.

Just then Todd appeared at the table with Enid, hoping that Jessica could provide some information about Elizabeth's whereabouts. He glanced around the table, surprised to find Jessica missing from her usual spot. "Hey, Lila, have you seen Jessica around?" Todd asked.

"Well, speak of the devil," said Caroline.

Lila shot her a dirty look. "No, we were just wondering where she was ourselves," she told Todd.

"Hmm, looks like both twins are missing in action," said Caroline. "Maybe Elizabeth's playing sick-nurse to her lovesick sister."

Todd stared at Caroline, aghast. How had she gotten this information? He looked at Enid quickly, but she shrugged, her expression as baffled as his. Had someone at the *Oracle* office heard them talking? He wanted to hit himself for being so indiscreet.

"Thanks, Lila," Todd said, heading off with Enid in tow. He didn't know why, but he had a gut instinct that something was wrong. Very wrong. And he had a feeling that it was more than a case of lovesickness.

"Well, that Jeremy Randall does seem to be the ladies' man these days, doesn't he?" said Ken.

"Yeah, I wonder who his next victim will be," said Amy. She looked around to make sure Todd was out of earshot. "Maybe Elizabeth's in love with Jeremy as well," she surmised. "That would explain why Todd Wilkins is running around the cafeteria like a chicken with its head cut off."

"Oh, really, Amy, that's impossible," Lila scoffed. "Jeremy is too slick for her. Mr. White Bread Wilkins is more her speed."

"Well, Elizabeth *was* wearing a black velvet cat suit last night," insisted Amy. "Maybe she got catty and jumped into the fray."

"Nah," said Lila, waving her hand dismissively. "Elizabeth came in costume, but Sue came dressed like herself—like the wicked witch she is." Lila picked up her Perrier with lime and took a sip through the straw. "Believe me, Sue's the one to worry about," she continued. "She's the witchy one." Lila said the words lightly, but for some reason a chill traveled slowly down her spine.

Chapter 6

Sue sat huddled on her knees on the round woven rug in the living room of the Nature Cabin, rubbing her hands briskly in front of the open fire. *I wonder what's going on at the Wakefields' now,* she thought, thinking of the cozy split-level home on Calico Drive. She was cold and lonely and filled with a sense of foreboding. Tiny red embers glowed in the fireplace. She tossed a handful of twigs into the crackling fire, watching as they flared up in a burst of orange and red.

Sue looked around the rustic room, searching for a way to occupy her time. Stripped of its festive Halloween decor, the cabin looked barren and dreary. Her eyes rested upon the cellular phone sitting in the middle of the room. She had brought it down with her in case Jeremy called. A sense of guilt coursed through her as she thought back to the phone call she had made earlier from the attic. She had dialed the Wakefields' number with trembling fingers, barely managing to press the play button on the tape recorder as she heard Ned Wakefield's strong voice come across the line. She had listened in silence as the menacing tape played, racked with guilt at the trouble she was causing the Wakefields.

The family must be terrified, she thought to herself. She could imagine how guilty Alice Wakefield felt, allowing her best friend's daughter to be abducted while in her care. Mrs. Wakefield had been through so much recently: the terrible loss of her best friend, Sue's failed wedding, and now this. And she had been so wonderful to Sue.

Sue stood up and paced the wooden floor, overcome with shame and regret. *This has gone too far,* she realized, blowing on her cold fingers. *And it's only going to get worse.* She sat down in a wooden rocking chair, deep in thought. Well, she determined finally, she was going to correct the situation before it deteriorated any further. When Jeremy came back, she would convince him that they had to give up their stupid plan—and her fortune as well. After all, her money was at stake, not Jeremy's, she reasoned. It was her decision to make. Sue rocked back and forth in the creaky chair, feeling a sense of peace wash over her for the first time in weeks.

Suddenly she heard the sounds of the lock turning in the front door. *Jeremy!* she thought in alarm, jumping out of the chair. He had given her strict orders not to leave the attic under any circumstances. But the cramped little chamber had been unbearable—full of dust and dirt and teeming with insects and bats. She dashed to the stairs and began quietly running up them. *Oh no!* she thought suddenly, stopping in the middle of the stairway. The kindled fire would give her away. She slid down onto a wooden stair and wrapped her arms around her knees, waiting nervously as Jeremy walked through the door.

Jeremy marched into the cabin, striding resolutely across the room. He paused perplexed in front of the flickering fire, then looked around the cabin quickly. As his eyes lit upon Sue perched on the staircase, his face slowly filled with anger. "What are you doing here?" he demanded harshly.

"I—I just—it was cold, and—" Sue stuttered.

"How dare you leave the attic! And light a fire! Do you want to get us both thrown in jail?" His voice was quaking with rage as he came toward her, an arm half-raised. His hulking figure cast an ominous shadow on the far wall. For a moment Sue thought he was going to hit her.

"Jeremy, I'm sorry!" Sue cried, cowering on the steps. "I thought I'd just come down here for a few minutes, just to warm up. . . ."

"Oh, I see!" said Jeremy, his voice dripping with sarcasm. "Spoiled little Susie Q wants half a million dollars, but she can't sit in an attic for an hour. Ohh, it's so *cold* and *cramped* up there." He spat out the words, his mouth twisting into an ugly sneer.

Sue dropped her face into her hands, a hot flush spreading across her pale cheeks. "Do you realize the risk that you've taken?" Jeremy asked, punctuating each word. He came toward her, continuing in a carefully controlled voice. "The Wakefields are going to send out a search party. And when they do, where do you think they are going to look first?"

Sue looked back at him, her eyes wide as saucers.

"Well, where?" he repeated, his voice rising.

"The . . . the cabin," Sue answered in a small voice.

"That's right, right here, the cabin. And what do you think you would have said if they'd stormed the place?" His voice changed, and he adopted a high-pitched, feminine tone. "Oh, hi, Mr. Wakefield. I thought I'd just light a cozy little fire while the kidnappers were out." Jeremy stomped to the fireplace and crushed the last of the burning embers with the solid heel of a hiking boot.

"You're right," Sue said, her voice pleading. "It was a stupid thing to do, and I promise it will never happen again. But, Jeremy, please calm down. *Nothing happened.*"

"This time," Jeremy snapped.

Sue hunched into the stairwell, tears trickling down her face. "Jeremy, I said I was sorry!" She buried her head in her hands and began crying in earnest.

Suddenly Jeremy was at her side, cradling her in his arms. "Sue, Sue, I'm sorry for yelling," he said, his voice gentle. He lifted her face to his and wiped the tears from her cheeks, trying to evoke a smile. "I guess the pressure's getting to both of us, hmm?" Sue smiled back at him, relieved that his anger had subsided.

"Oh, Jeremy," Sue sighed, cuddling in his arms. "Let's not go through with this. Look what it's doing to us. Our love is more important than any amount of money could be."

"Sue, what are you saying?" Jeremy asked. Sue looked up at him quickly, trying to gauge his expression. He looked calm and rational and was looking at her with an earnest expression on his face.

Sue took a deep breath and plunged ahead. "I've been thinking about this for a while. I—I don't think we should go through with the plan," she said. "It's too dangerous. We could get into serious trouble."

"I'm afraid it's too late to get cold feet now," said Jeremy. "We're in too deep to back out."

"Jeremy, we still have time to undo what we've done," Sue said, choosing her words carefully. "I could just show up at the Wakefields' today. I would say that I had been held hostage at the cabin. And that I escaped."

But Jeremy was shaking his head. "It's too risky. They'd check out the story," Jeremy said. "They'd come back here looking for the kidnapper, and they'd search for him—until they found him—*us*. No, we've got to be safely out of the country before that search takes place."

"But there must be some way to get out of it," Sue protested. "I feel so guilty," she admitted. "The Wakefields have been so kind to me. Alice and Ned have treated me like a daughter, and Elizabeth is like a sister to me."

"Sue," Jeremy said, "we've already set the plan in motion. We've got no choice but to follow it through." A look of steely determination had settled over his face. Sue stared at the floor, looking downcast. "And besides," he reminded her, "we're not really doing anything wrong. The money is rightfully

67

yours. We're only doing this so we can be together, comfortably. After all, either we live together in poverty—or I spend the rest of my life with Jessica Wakefield."

Sue fell silent, unable to think of any further arguments. *The money is rightfully ours,* she repeated to herself, trying to be convinced by his words.

"What is wrong with this machine?" Jeremy growled, hitting the side of the old tape recorder. He punched the play and record buttons at the same time, snarling with frustration as the tape stood still.

Sue watched Jeremy with alarm. It wasn't like him to get so worked up. Jeremy was usually so calm and gentle. And he was always patient in difficult situations. Well, maybe he was feeling guilty about everything, too, thought Sue to herself. She reached out and touched his arm. "Jeremy, maybe the batteries are out," she ventured softly.

Jeremy turned the machine over and yanked open the cartridge at the back, flipping two small batteries onto the ground. He stomped to the closet and pulled out a tool kit, rummaging through it furiously until he came up with a package of fresh batteries. He inserted the new set into the machine and hit the buttons violently again. "Beautiful," he breathed with a smile as the tape began to wind slowly in its socket.

"OK, sweetheart, time for part two," Jeremy said, rubbing his hands together. "This time we up the ante by a hundred thousand dollars."

"What?" Sue exclaimed.

"The ransom is now officially six hundred thousand

68

dollars for the much-desired, long-lost Sue Gibbons. And I think she's worth it, don't you?" He leaned over to kiss her on the cheek, but she backed away.

"But, Jeremy, why?" Sue responded, stunned at the idea.

"The Wakefields have hired a detective, that's why," Jeremy explained, his eyes glinting sharply. "They were warned not to contact the authorities."

"But we don't need more money!" Sue cried.

"No, but we've got to make sure they don't call the police next time," explained Jeremy. He stopped the tape and began to rewind it. "Besides, ol' Ned's a lawyer," continued Jeremy glibly. He laughed a short, brusque laugh. "He can afford it."

"Jeremy!" Sue began to protest, but he cut her short.

"Sue, we haven't got much time," he said, turning his attention back to the tape recorder.

Sue shivered as Jeremy made the new recording. He was beginning to scare her. He seemed like a total stranger, hunched over the machine with a handkerchief covering his mouth as he spoke in an evil voice. Jeremy's behavior seemed completely out of character. He had never cared about money before. He had said all along that he only wanted her to have the inheritance that was rightfully hers. But then why was he demanding even more money?

Jeremy clicked the stop button and rewound the tape, listening to the recording carefully. He smiled with satisfaction at the final words.

He picked up the tape recorder and tucked it under his arm. "OK, Susie Q, back to your hideout," he said gently, ushering Sue to the second floor. After she had left the room, he grabbed a rickety wooden chair with his free hand and followed her upstairs.

Sue climbed the flimsy ladder leading to the attic and sat down dispiritedly on a rolled-up carpet. Jeremy followed her up, depositing the chair and tape recorder on the deck. Sue took in the familiar surroundings, dismayed to be cooped up in her dreary hideaway again. Then her eyes widened in terror as she saw Jeremy propping up the chair and unwinding a large coil of rope. "Jeremy, what—what are you doing?" she asked.

"I'm afraid we're going to have to tie you up this time," Jeremy said, threading the rope around the back of the chair.

"But I said I wouldn't leave the attic again." Sue's heart pounded in her chest. "Don't you believe me?" Now she felt frightened for real. What was happening to Jeremy?

"Of course I do," said Jeremy, laughing softly. "It's just a precaution. If someone found you here, it would look suspicious. They would question why you hadn't managed to escape. So we've got to make it look like you couldn't get out."

"You're right," Sue agreed, nodding her head unhappily. Jeremy's words made sense. The Nature Cabin was the most logical place to look for her. And even though the trapdoor was pretty well concealed, it could still be detected.

"Don't worry," Jeremy said. "It won't be long. And I'll come back and check on you periodically."

Jeremy patted the seat of the chair, and Sue sat

down on it reluctantly. He looped the cord around her waist several times and fastened it securely to the back of the chair. "OK?" Jeremy asked. Sue nodded her head in a stoic manner. Then he tied her arms together behind her back and bound her feet firmly to the legs of the chair. Sue tried to flex her wrists. She could already feel the ropes cutting into her circulation.

Jeremy fished around in a dusty chest and pulled out a red bandanna. "Wait!" Sue cried as he came toward her with it. She was overcome with a sense of panic. She didn't know how she could endure being tied up for hours while Jeremy was gone. It was bad enough being locked up alone in the attic.

"What is it?" he asked. She could sense the impatience in his eyes.

"Jeremy," she said, thinking quickly, "if I'm tied up here, I won't be able to call the Wakefields this evening."

"Don't worry, I've thought of that," Jeremy said. He climbed down the attic steps and returned moments later carrying the cellular phone. He placed the phone and tape recorder on a low shelf by her back and slightly loosened the cord binding her right hand. "Now see if you can hit the buttons." Sue twisted her head around and stretched out the fingers on her right hand, just reaching the phone. "Perfect," Jeremy breathed. "This will give you just enough leeway to dial the number, but not enough to escape." Sue's heart pounded in her chest. Was Jeremy trying to make it *look* as if she couldn't escape, or was he actually trying to prevent her from escaping?

71

Jeremy dropped a light cloth next to the phone. "Now, as soon as you've made the call, drape this over the phone and the tape recorder," he commanded.

Sue just nodded, her eyes wide.

Jeremy carefully covered her mouth with the bandanna, knotting it tightly at the back of her head. "'Bye, sweetheart," he said softly, leaning over and kissing her lightly on the cheek. He pulled down the shade on the tiny window, and darkness filled the room.

"And remember, five o'clock," he said on his way out. He turned back at the foot of the stairs. "And don't blow it." The trapdoor slammed shut.

A tremor ran down Sue's body after Jeremy left the cabin. She fought down the rising tide of panic that threatened to engulf her. Bound to the chair in the pitch-black attic, she could barely move, breathe, or see. Sue forced herself to stay calm while her eyes adapted to the dim light. It was early in the morning, but it seemed like the dead of night in the dusky attic.

As soon as her surroundings became more visible, Sue pulled at the ropes wrapped around her, trying to ascertain how securely she was bound. She was tied so tightly that she could hardly shift at all in the hard wooden seat. But the worst part was the bandanna biting into her lips. She felt as if she would suffocate with the handkerchief wrapped around her face, preventing her from breathing. She jerked her head repeatedly, steadily loosening the handkerchief until it fell underneath her chin. Then she took a deep breath, savoring the feel of the air circulating freely. Well, she decided, she would just tell Jeremy it fell off. Maybe she could unfasten the ropes too. She would tighten them again when Jeremy came back. She wrenched her body in the seat, trying to loosen the cords attaching her torso to the chair. They didn't give. Frustrated, she yanked at the ropes on her wrists and ankles, pulling with all her might. Finally, her body sore and her shoulders aching, she abandoned her efforts.

For the first time since she had been with Jeremy, Sue questioned her judgment. Maybe Jeremy wasn't the person she thought he was. Her mother had never approved of him. She hadn't believed that he loved her. *Believe me, Sue,* she could hear her mother saying, *he only wants you for your fortune.* Sue had dismissed her mother's words. Jeremy had seemed so kind and loving and generous. But now she wasn't so sure.

What have I gotten myself into? Sue asked herself in distress. She thought back to how the whole thing had started, to that summer day a few months ago. It had all been Jeremy's idea. "Let's go to Sweet Valley. . . ." he had said. Sue had been hesitant at first. She wanted to respect her mother's last wishes. But Jeremy had convinced her that the money was rightfully hers. And then he had come up with an elaborate plan. . . .

Sue sighed, shifting uncomfortably on the hard, splintery seat. If only she could turn back the clock. She longed to return to the innocence of that hot summer in Manhattan, before she and Jeremy had gotten involved with Sweet Valley and the Wakefields and crime.

Sue couldn't remember ever being so physically uncomfortable, not even when she and Jeremy had gone on a safari in the steaming African jungle. The cords binding her wrists and ankles were cutting into the bone, digging ugly red welts in her tender skin. Her shoulders were aching from her hands' being tied behind her. And her back was stiff and sore from her upright position in the hard wooden chair. She longed to get up and walk around. Her eyelids fluttered shut as she leaned her head back wearily against the wall.

Sue heard a noise coming from the cabin's first floor and opened her eyes quickly. She sat perfectly still, barely breathing. What would she do if they found her here? She listened carefully, waiting for the sound to repeat. She realized with relief that it was just water running through the pipes. Suddenly Sue was hit by the magnitude of what she and Jeremy were doing. The stakes were much higher than she'd originally realized. If they were caught, they could be put in prison. Sue was amazed at their audacity. How could she and Jeremy have planned to take on Ned Wakefield, one of the most renowned lawyers in southern California? Now she felt foolish for thinking she could trick the Wakefields. And Elizabeth felt like a sister to her. Elizabeth had been such a supportive friend through everything, thought Sue guiltily, remembering her rare blood disease. Elizabeth had been entirely forgiving when Sue had told her the truth about the illness. Elizabeth had just been happy to know her friend was healthy.

Sue wiggled uncomfortably in the rigid chair, wondering how she had gotten herself so far into this and how she could possibly get herself out. But she also felt afraid of Jeremy somehow, afraid to back out now.

And all for her mother's money, thought Sue sadly. Until now she had believed her actions were justified. After all, her mother shouldn't have tried to keep her from the person she loved. But now she saw Jeremy in a new light. She conjured up an image of her mother, feeling an intense mixture of grief and guilt. Maybe her mother had been right, after all.

Chapter 7

"I'll get it!" said Elizabeth when the doorbell rang. She hurried to the front of the house to let Detective Diamond in.

Elizabeth opened the door and stared speechless at the attractive woman standing on the doorstep.

"Hi. I'm Sam Diamond," said the detective, putting out her hand.

"Sam?" said Elizabeth as she shook the woman's hand.

"Samantha, actually," said the detective, smiling warmly. "But all my friends call me Sam."

"Oh! Well, I'm Elizabeth," said Elizabeth. "Please come in," she added quickly, realizing that Detective Diamond was still standing on the doorstep.

"Hello, Sam!" said Ned as the detective walked into the foyer. "Alice! Sam's here," he called.

Mrs. Wakefield walked quickly into the vestibule. "Sam, how are you?" Alice said, clasping the other woman's hand warmly. "Thank you so much for coming on such short notice."

"It's my pleasure," said Sam. "It's been too long, anyway. I'm thrilled to have the chance to finally meet your family."

"You've met Elizabeth?" inquired Mrs. Wakefield.

"Yes, we introduced ourselves," said Sam. "But I would have recognized her on the street. She looks just like you."

"That's what I like to hear," said Mrs. Wakefield, her eyes dancing merrily.

"Jessica!" Mr. Wakefield called.

"Coming, coming," muttered Jessica, making her way grumpily down the steps. She stopped suddenly at the sight of the detective, staring at the elegant young woman in amazement. With her short-cropped blond hair and winter-white Chanel suit, Sam Diamond looked more like a fashion consultant than a private detective.

"Two of them!" Sam exclaimed, looking from Jessica to Elizabeth.

"Yes, two of them. Sometimes they're quite a handful," said Mrs. Wakefield wryly. "Sam, this is Jessica," she said, turning to her daughter. *The evil twin,* thought Jessica.

"Hi, Jessica. Nice to meet you," said Sam, giving her a friendly smile.

"She's a woman!" exclaimed Jessica to Elizabeth after her parents and Sam had retreated to the study to confer about the case.

"That's very astute of you, Jess," teased Elizabeth.

"Thanks, Liz," responded Jessica, plopping down onto the bottom step. "What I mean is, she's a woman *detective*," she amended.

"Jessica!" Elizabeth admonished. "Why shouldn't she be a woman?"

"Detectives are always men," explained Jessica, ticking them off on her fingers. "Inspector Clouseau, Hercule Poirot, Philip Marlowe, Sherlock Holmes . . ."

"And what about Nancy Drew and Miss Marple?" demanded Elizabeth, her hands on her hips. "Or Lucy Friday, the crime editor at the *London Journal*?"

"That's different," scoffed Jessica. "Lucy Friday *reported* on crimes. She didn't *solve* them."

Elizabeth rolled her eyes in exasperation. "Jessica, that's not the point!"

"What is the point?" asked Jessica.

"The point is that the gender of the detective is irrelevant. She can do everything a man can," asserted Elizabeth. "And more!"

"I didn't say she couldn't," responded Jessica. "But I don't know how she'd make an arrest or protect herself in those heels."

"Jessica, she's a private detective, not an FBI agent," replied Elizabeth. "If she was involved in a dangerous situation, she would use a gun. Just like a man."

Jessica looked unconvinced. "Well, if she's some roving detective, then why does she look like she should be on the cover of *Vogue*?"

"Are you saying that I shouldn't be able to have a career as a writer or a journalist just because I look

like I could be on the cover of a fashion mag—?"
Elizabeth stopped midsentence.

Jessica smiled at her sister's comment. "So you
think you look like a model, Liz?" she asked, a twin-
kle in her blue-green eyes.

"No, no, that's not what I meant," said Elizabeth,
her face flushing. "I just meant that a woman's looks
shouldn't affect her career."

"Hmm," said Jessica, gazing critically at her twin
image. "You *do* look like you could be on the cover of
Vogue. Well, maybe *Sweet Sixteen*," she said teas-
ingly. "Good idea, Liz. Maybe we should consider a
career in modeling. After all, we were chosen to do a
fashion spread for *Sweet Sixteen* before the Jungle
Prom. What do you think? Jessica and Elizabeth
Wakefield—Supermodel Twins." She paused, testing
out the sound of the new title. "Maybe you should
change your name, though. How about Jessica and
Jocelyn? Or Jessica and Jacqueline? Or just Jess and
Jackie? Elizabeth, what do you think of 'Jackie'?"

But Elizabeth was just staring at her twin in
amazement, wondering how they could have been
cast from the same mold. The last thing on earth
she'd want to spend her life doing was standing in
front of a camera like a pretty object. How could
Jessica completely lack any feminist consciousness?
wondered Elizabeth. But, then, it wasn't that surprising, considering the fact that Jessica was engaged to
be married at the age of sixteen. Elizabeth sighed
audibly, worried about her twin. Was Jessica just
going to throw away her whole life and future for
some man?

"Well, Jacqueline?" prodded Jessica.

"Jessica, you're impossible!" Elizabeth finally spluttered.

"Well, just think about it," said Jessica with an impish grin. "Jackie!"

"Girls!" came the sound of Mrs. Wakefield's voice. "Join us in the living room. We're having a meeting."

"Oh, great," said Jessica, getting up reluctantly. "A family powwow." She twirled her finger in the air and followed Elizabeth down the hall.

"OK, this will enable us to record and trace all incoming calls," said Sam, setting up an elaborate phone system, complete with a radio transmitter and a high-tech reel-to-reel tape recorder.

Elizabeth sucked in her breath as she took in the elaborate array of electronic devices. "Wow, that's a pretty complicated system," she said, giving her sister a pointed look. Jessica shrugged and looked away.

"What I'd like to do first is interview each of you individually to get all the information about the case," said Sam in a businesslike tone. "Do I have your consent to record the conversation?" She looked around as everybody nodded.

"OK, Alice, we'll start with you," said Sam, pressing the record button on a miniature tape recorder. "Now, what is your relationship to Sue Gibbons?"

Alice began recounting her friendship with Sue's family, but the sound of the doorbell interrupted her.

"It's Jeremy!" Jessica squealed, jumping up and flying down the hall. She practically ran into Jeremy as he opened the door himself.

"Whoa! Hold on there," he said, laughing as Jessica barged into his arms. "What's up, Jess?"

"Oh, Jeremy," Jessica cried, snuggling up to him. "It's been so awful here! I wanted to talk to you, and I tried to get hold of you, but—but you weren't there." She bit her lip and looked up at him anxiously. It seemed as if he'd been avoiding her lately, and she was desperate for some reassurance.

"What time did you call?" asked Jeremy.

"Oh, I don't know," said Jessica, forcing her tone to sound casual. "I guess it was—around ninish." *The time of your conference call*, said a voice in her head.

"Oh, well, you must have called during my conference call," Jeremy said in an offhand tone.

Jessica hesitated. She didn't want to sound like a carping wife, but he hadn't provided a satisfactory explanation. "But I thought you have call waiting," she persisted.

"Well, you know I couldn't interrupt the call," explained Jeremy, his voice lightly reproaching. "I *wondered* who kept calling."

"Oh, Jeremy, I'm sorry," said Jessica. She felt silly for having questioned him. And she was embarrassed to seem so needy and dependent. She didn't want to come off like the pathetic clinging vine that Sue had been. "I thought that maybe the call was finished. I didn't mean to bother you."

"Don't worry about it, sweetheart," said Jeremy, bending down to plant a warm kiss on her lips. "You could never bother me."

❖　　❖　　❖

"Jeremy's here!" said Jessica, proudly leading Jeremy into the room like a prize trophy.

"We can see that, Jessica," said Mr. Wakefield dryly. "Jeremy, this is Sam Diamond," he said, introducing him to the detective.

Elizabeth studied Jeremy as he shook the detective's hand firmly. *What is it about him?* she wondered. He always acted perfectly proper and polite. *There is something a little too smooth about him,* she decided. She scrutinized his face and clothes but couldn't find any clue in his appearance. His handsome face was like a mask. *Covering what?* wondered Elizabeth to herself. Well, she decided with determination, maybe this case called for *two* women detectives. "I'll be right back," Elizabeth said suddenly, jumping up and running to her room to get a notebook.

When she returned carrying a small spiral notebook, Mrs. Wakefield was in the process of explaining her relationship with Nancy Gibbons.

". . . so I wanted to help Sue with her wedding . . . for Nancy," Mrs. Wakefield was saying. "But then, then . . ." Alice's voice broke off as her eyes filled with tears. Elizabeth looked up from her notebook, troubled to see her mother looking so distraught. She knew her mother believed she had failed in her goal to help her dear friend.

"I think that's enough," said Sam sympathetically as Ned put a comforting arm around his wife's shoulders. Jessica squirmed uncomfortably and sank down into the big armchair she was curled up in.

"So what happened with the wedding?" Sam inquired, directing her question at Mr. Wakefield.

"Why don't we let Jessica take that question?" suggested Mr. Wakefield. Jessica's face flushed as Sam turned her attention to her.

"OK. Jessica, let's turn to you. Now, how would you describe your relationship with Sue Gibbons?" asked Sam.

"Well, Sue and I became pretty good friends when she came to stay with us to prepare for her wedding. We spent a lot of time together—Sue and Liz and I—shopping and going to the beach and stuff." Jessica swallowed hard before continuing. "But about a week before her arrival, I was on the beach with my friend Lila, when . . ."

Elizabeth listened with interest as Jessica began presenting her side of the story. She wondered how her sister was going to justify her actions.

"And then I met this god, I mean this boy, I mean Jeremy, on the beach," said Jessica, her face flushing. "And I knew right then and there that he was the man for me. He was the person I had been waiting for my whole life." Elizabeth groaned inwardly. How could Jessica say she had been spent her entire life waiting for a man?

"But then he disappeared, saying we could never be together," Jessica continued. "And the next thing I knew, I found out that the man of my dreams just happened to be, well, the same man that Sue had been raving about."

The detective's eyes widened at this point, but she didn't say anything. *What a tale!* thought Elizabeth to herself, quickly recording her sister's words and the detective's reaction.

"But we didn't want to hurt Sue. So we vowed to avoid one another. We tried as hard as we could to keep away from each other," Jessica said, looking at Jeremy for confirmation. He nodded and took her hand. *You tried as hard as you could to see each other is more like it*, thought Elizabeth, thinking back to all the secret rendezvous Jessica and Jeremy managed to have behind Sue's back.

"But, well, no matter how hard we tried, no matter how hard we resisted, we just couldn't stay away from each other. We couldn't deny our love," Jessica finished softly.

"So then you called the wedding off?" inquired the detective, looking at Jeremy.

"Well, Jeremy was planning to marry Sue anyway," Jessica said, fielding the question. "He felt he couldn't leave her because of her disease."

"Her disease?" questioned Sam.

"What disease?" demanded Mrs. Wakefield, looking perplexed.

"Well, Sue felt a little, ah, desperate, about the situation with Jeremy, so she claimed to have the same rare blood disease that killed her mother in order to keep Jeremy with her," explained Elizabeth quickly, trying to tone down the story. They had promised Sue they wouldn't tell anyone about it, but it was probably just as well for everybody to know the truth. Sue was in serious danger, and Sam needed to have all the facts to solve this crime.

"And her little scheme worked," Jessica said, an edge to her voice. "Sue knew how generous and altruistic Jeremy is. And she played on those feelings.

Considering the situation, he didn't feel he could abandon her. So he decided to sacrifice his own happiness for hers." Jessica paused, her eyes shining with love for her hero. *I think I'm going to vomit*, thought Elizabeth.

"Well, this is the first I've heard of all this," said Mrs. Wakefield. "May I ask why we weren't informed?"

Elizabeth turned guilty eyes to her mother. "She asked us to keep it a secret. I guess she was embarrassed."

"Well, I can't say I blame her," said Mr. Wakefield, shaking his head.

"So how was the situation finally resolved?" asked the detective.

"Well, true love won out in the end," Jessica said simply.

"And how did that happen?" Sam asked skeptically.

"Well, I stopped the wedding," Jessica explained.

"You—stopped the wedding? Before it happened, I presume," said Sam.

"Well, no, actually, while it was happening," said Jessica. Elizabeth noticed her mother's face turn a dark shade of red.

"While it was happening," the detective repeated. "And how exactly did you accomplish that?"

"Well, when the minister said for anyone who objected to the marriage to speak now or forever hold their peace, I, uh, spoke," Jessica explained. "Like they say, all's fair in love and war, right?"

Sam lifted an eyebrow but declined to comment.

A heavy silence hung over the room after Jessica

made her confession. Elizabeth coughed. "How about some iced tea?" she suggested, trying to break the tension in the room.

"Good idea, Liz," said Mr. Wakefield.

"I'll help you," squeaked Jessica, following her sister into the kitchen.

Jessica and Elizabeth returned a few minutes later with a tray of iced tea and a platter of crackers and cheese.

"Why don't we turn to you next, Elizabeth?" suggested Sam as Elizabeth laid the platter on the coffee table.

"Sure," agreed Elizabeth, sitting down with an iced tea.

"Your mother tells me you and Sue have developed quite a close friendship," began the detective. Elizabeth nodded. "Do you have any insights into the situation at hand?" she inquired.

Elizabeth pondered the question thoughtfully, wondering how much information to offer. "Well," she said carefully, "I think the situation is very serious, and I'm concerned that Sue's in great danger . . ."

"But—?" pressed Sam.

"But, well, I think we should also consider the possibility that this is a scam," Elizabeth said. She lifted her iced tea to her lips.

"And what would make you draw that conclusion?" asked Sam.

Elizabeth paused. She didn't want to implicate Sue, but she felt it was her duty to throw out the possibility that all of this had been Sue's doing. "Well, I know Sue felt desperate at the thought of losing Jeremy. And

87

she took some rash measures to keep him."

"Like the faked rare blood disease," put in the detective.

"And her suicide attempt following the wedding," added Mrs. Wakefield.

"Exactly." Elizabeth nodded. "So maybe in this case it's possible that she, that she . . ." Elizabeth spread her hands out in a wide gesture, hesitant to finish her thought.

"That she orchestrated the kidnapping in order to regain Jeremy's affections," concluded Sam.

"Right," said Elizabeth. She wondered if she should bring up the light she had seen in the cabin the night before. She opened her mouth to mention the strange occurrence but stopped herself. Her parents didn't know that they had been out in the woods the night before. And besides, she had been almost out of her head with fear. She was probably just imagining things in her frightened state.

"That's ridiculous!" said Jeremy. Elizabeth jumped at the unexpected intrusion of Jeremy's strong voice into her thoughts. "Sue may have taken some drastic measures in the past, but she would never go this far. She is extremely grateful to your family for all you have done—she would never put you in this position."

"It's important that we consider all the possibilities, no matter how outlandish they may sound," said Sam calmly.

"But Sue's in grave danger!" protested Jeremy, his voice bubbling forth with emotion. "If we waste our time investigating the *ridiculous* possibility that this is some scam, we'll allow the kidnapper to gain the upper hand." Elizabeth looked at Jeremy curiously. Why was he reacting so strongly to the notion that the kidnapping was a scam? He was probably just overly protective about Sue, she decided. After all, they had once been engaged to be married.

"Jeremy, we have to investigate every lead in this case precisely because of its serious nature," said Sam firmly. "Now, Elizabeth, could you describe your friendship with Sue?" she asked.

"Well, we weren't really close at first," admitted Elizabeth. "I didn't particularly like her because she was so focused on material objects. But then it became clear that Sue's materialism was a result of her insecurity. And it all made sense to me in the end when I found out about Sue's inheritance."

"Sue's inheritance?" Sam inquired.

"Sue's mother didn't approve of Jeremy, so she left her inheritance to me," Mrs. Wakefield explained. "But Nancy had stipulated in her will that if Sue and Jeremy ever broke up, the money was to return to Sue after a two-month period. And as they— well, broke off their engagement on September first, the money is legally Sue's on November first."

"Today," said Sam.

"Yes," said Alice.

Elizabeth caught Jessica's eye and Jessica shook her head no. After Jessica had caught Jeremy with Sue the night before, it had occurred to both of them that Sue would no longer get her inheritance. But then it turned out that Jeremy and Sue hadn't gotten back together after all. *Jeremy cleared all that up last night,* thought Elizabeth. *Didn't he?*

"Thank you, Elizabeth," said Sam. "This has been very helpful. Now, Jeremy, do you concur so far with all the information that has been relayed today?"

"Yes, I do," Jeremy said, nodding his head seriously.

"So as I understand it, you and Sue were willing to forgo Sue's fortune in order to get married, is that correct?" asked Sam.

"Yes, she felt that I was more important than her fortune," said Jeremy in an even tone. "And the money didn't mean anything to me."

"And do you know of anybody else who would have been aware of Sue's inheritance?" asked Sam. "Friends of Sue, family members?"

"Yes, I do," said Jeremy. His voice shook with anger as he spoke. "I'm certain that Sue's stepfather, Phil, is behind this. He was always resentful that Mrs. Gibbons wasn't leaving the money to him. He felt that he deserved it."

Elizabeth watched Jeremy closely as he spoke. The anger in his voice seemed genuine, yet something didn't click.

"And now he's trying to get the money in the most despicable way," continued Jeremy, his voice barely suppressing rage.

"His name is Phil Gibbons?" Sam asked.

"No, Phil Schmitt. Sue's mother kept her original married name when she got remarried," Jeremy explained.

"Can you tell me anything about his relationship with Nancy and Sue?" asked Sam, scribbling his name on a yellow legal pad.

"Well, he was married to Sue's mother for about eight years, so he was really like a surrogate father to Sue. In name at least," Jeremy said.

Sam's eyebrows shot up and she looked at Jeremy inquiringly.

"Well," Jeremy explained, "he wasn't much of a father to Sue. I think he would have preferred to have Nancy all to himself."

"But he was at the wedding, right?" inquired Sam.

"He gave her away," jumped in Elizabeth. "Or— at least he tried to," she added lamely.

Jeremy scoffed. "I'm sure he just came out of duty. Or maybe he had some *business* to attend to in L.A."

"You know," Elizabeth said thoughtfully, "Mr. Schmitt was very nice at the wedding, but he left immediately following the ceremony. And after Sue's suicide attempt he said he was too busy to fly back from New York. He didn't seem overly concerned."

"I see," said Sam. Elizabeth looked at the detective closely, trying to gauge whether or not she considered Phil Schmitt a possible suspect, but it was impossible to read her face.

"Now, Jeremy, could you tell us about your relationship to Sue?" Sam inquired.

"Sue's been like a sister to me—and that's all she's ever been," said Jeremy, his tone changing rapidly from anger to regret. "I never should have let her talk me into getting engaged," he said, shaking his head sadly. "I just ended up hurting her more." He looked down for a moment. "It's Jessica I love," he said finally, looking over at Jessica and sending her a tender look. "But I would die if anything happened to Sue," he added.

Elizabeth watched carefully as Jeremy made this tearful speech, but instead of being moved, chills ran down her spine.

Sam stood up abruptly and slapped her book shut, causing Elizabeth to jump.

"Well, I think I've got enough for the moment," she said. "Thank you all for your cooperation. Ned, I'd like to go through my notes and make some phone calls. Do you think I could use the study?"

"Certainly," said Ned, jumping up to escort her to his office. Sam turned and walked out of the room but stopped and turned back in the entranceway. "And one more thing," she said, her voice grave. "It's imperative that you don't let anybody know what's going on here, and I mean *anybody*."

"Did you get that, girls?" repeated Ned, looking pointedly at Jessica. The girls nodded their heads.

"Or you could jeopardize Sue's life," Sam added, and shut the door.

Chapter 8

"Jessica, I've *got* to talk to you," said Elizabeth, who had been holed up in her room for the past two hours, going over her notes about the case. She had run the facts through her mind again and again, but no matter how hard she tried, she couldn't make sense of the information. Something about this kidnapping didn't fit. Something seemed suspicious.

"Liz, do you mind? I'm watching a rerun of *Three's Company*," complained Jessica. She was sprawled out on the family-room couch, one foot peeking out of a woolen afghan.

"*Three's Company*? Where's Jeremy?" asked Elizabeth.

"Very funny, Liz. He said he had to get back to his room to do some stupid environmental work," grumbled Jessica.

"Jess, I think we should talk about the case now that we have some time alone," Elizabeth said, her voice urgent. She looked around quickly to make sure no one was in earshot. "I think something's really fishy."

Jessica rolled her eyes. "Don't you think one dazzling detective is enough?"

Elizabeth refused to rise to the bait. "Jessica, I want to talk," she said, her voice determined.

"OK, OK," said Jessica. "But can you just wait till the show is over?"

"Jessica, I've been waiting all day!" Elizabeth said, hauling her sister off the couch and pulling her up the steps to Jessica's bedroom.

"Geez!" exclaimed Jessica when she got into her room, collapsing into a pile of clothes strewn across the floor. She rubbed her arm briskly. "Did you have to pull my arm off?"

"Sorry," said Elizabeth. "But I'm concerned about this case." She climbed into Jessica's bed and propped herself up against the wall, drawing her knees up to her chest. "I just don't want you to get hurt."

"Me?" exclaimed Jessica. "What do I have to do with it?"

Elizabeth hesitated, reluctant to voice her suspicions to her sister. "Jess," she finally blurted out, "I'm worried about you. I don't think Jeremy can be trusted."

"Oh, great," Jessica said, "we're going to play 'Jump on Jeremy' again. Liz, I'm getting tired of this game."

"Jessica, if this is a game, I don't want to see you losing. A guy who cheated on his fiancée would cheat on you too," Elizabeth said, her voice insistent.

"Oh, Liz," Jessica scoffed. "He only lied to Sue because he thought she had a fatal disease. Otherwise, he would have called the whole thing off."

"But, Jess, what about before that? He cheated on Sue from the day he met you," Elizabeth pointed out.

"So? Is it Jeremy's fault that he fell in love with me?" responded Jessica. "Are you saying that it's not possible for Jeremy to be truly and totally in love with me?"

"No, of course it's possible," said Elizabeth. "But on the other hand, maybe he is just a Casanova who likes to play the field."

"Well, you're going to have to come up with some stronger evidence," scoffed Jessica, rapidly losing patience. "Face it, Elizabeth, you've always been against my relationship with Jeremy. You don't approve of him because you think he's too old, so you're trying to turn me against him. And I'm getting sick of it. I'm sick of your insults about Jeremy, and I'm sick of your holier-than-thou attitude," Jessica said, her voice rising rapidly. "Why can't you just be happy for me?"

Elizabeth wanted to scream. Couldn't Jessica see that she wasn't judging her, that she was just concerned about her well-being? Elizabeth took a deep breath. Despite Jessica's outburst, she had to forge ahead. She had to voice her concerns. "Jessica," Elizabeth said softly, "I would like more than anything to trust Jeremy. But I just think there are a few too many odd coincidences in this case."

"Like what?" demanded Jessica.

"Well, like the fact that you caught Jeremy with

Sue at the Halloween party *exactly* two months after they broke up."

"I did not catch Jeremy with Sue," said Jessica hotly. "He was just comforting her."

"OK, OK—maybe," said Elizabeth. "But just follow the logic through for a second."

"Which is?" Jessica stared at her sister, her arms folded stubbornly across her chest.

"Which is—that maybe Jeremy and Sue just broke up so Sue could get her inheritance. And then they could run away together or something." Elizabeth stared at her sister anxiously, afraid that her suggestion might send Jessica over the edge.

"Elizabeth," said Jessica, her voice calm and even, "you would have a very interesting theory, except for one thing. One little thing."

"What's that?" asked Elizabeth.

"Jeremy didn't break up with Sue. And Sue didn't break up with Jeremy. I broke up the wedding, remember?"

Elizabeth was silent. Jessica had a point— Elizabeth's logic was flawed. Jeremy and Sue couldn't have orchestrated their breakup in order to gain Sue's fortune. *Maybe I'm getting paranoid,* Elizabeth thought. But, still . . .

"OK, Jess," Elizabeth conceded, "forget about the Jeremy thing. Forgive me for my suspicions. But what do you think about the strange coincidence of events in Sue's kidnapping?"

"Like the fact that you lost your mind on exactly the same day that Sue got kidnapped?" Jessica asked.

Elizabeth, too distracted to defend herself,

leafed through her notebook and jumped off Jessica's bed, pacing back and forth through piles of clothing and magazines. "What about the fact that the amount of the ransom equals Sue's inheritance exactly? And that the date of the kidnapping coincides exactly with the date Sue was to have received her money. And—"

Suddenly the phone jangled, interrupting Elizabeth's litany. Jessica picked it up. "Oh, hi, Todd," she said warmly. For the first time in her life, Jessica was glad to hear Todd's voice so she could get Elizabeth off her back. "Just a sec, Todd," she said brightly, waiting while Elizabeth scrambled into her room. Jessica returned the receiver to the cradle as she heard her sister's voice breathlessly answer the phone.

"Todd!" Elizabeth said, relieved to hear his voice. "Where are you?"

"Where am I? Where do you think I am? The same place I always am on Monday at three o'clock," said Todd.

"Oh, that's right, school," Elizabeth said, her tone serious.

"Hey, Liz, what's going on? Why are you and Jessica at home?" Todd asked. "Is something wrong?"

"Oh, no, no, nothing's wrong," Elizabeth said, attempting to sound casual but only managing a squeak. "We just felt a little under the weather after the party. I guess maybe we were out too late," she explained weakly.

"But you left the party early," protested Todd.

"Uh, right," Elizabeth responded, unable to come up with another explanation.

"Hey, what's the matter?" Todd asked, trying to lighten the atmosphere. "I thought we were all back to normal since I removed all my unsightly, excess facial hair." Todd had adopted a new hairstyle and had attempted to grow a mustache. Elizabeth had found both the long hair flipping over Todd's eyes and the short peach fuzz adorning his upper lip horrendous. His whole personality had seemed to change, and they had almost broken up because of it.

"We are!" said Elizabeth, forcing a laugh. "Now that you've given up on the Charlie Chaplin thing, everything's back to the way it was." She tried to sound light, but her voice was leaden. "Yep, a return to normalcy for Todd and Elizabeth." *Normalcy!* she thought with a laugh.

"Liz, if everything is so normal, then why are you acting so strange?" pressed Todd.

Elizabeth leaned her head against the wall. Obviously, her efforts weren't working. She realized she had to hang up or she would tell Todd everything. "Todd, I better go," she said quickly.

"Elizabeth, why?" Elizabeth could hear real concern is his voice. "Liz, what's going on?"

"Todd, it's nothing," Elizabeth insisted, forcing a note of annoyance into her voice. "I just don't feel well, OK? I need to take a nap. Can't we just talk later?"

"OK, Liz, I'll talk to you later," said Todd. "I love you," he added softly.

"I love you," Elizabeth returned.

"OK, 'bye," Todd said.

Elizabeth heard the phone click off. "'Bye," she whispered into the receiver. She coiled the phone cord around her hand, wishing desperately that she could tell Todd what was going on so she wouldn't feel so alone.

Chapter 9

"So the word around school is that Jessica caught Jeremy and Sue together—in the woods last night," Lila confided to Robby in a low voice. Lila and Robby were sharing an ice-cream sundae and a float at Casey's Ice Cream Parlor on Monday after school.

"Wow," Robby said, whistling softly under his breath. He took a long draw on the root-beer float and shook his head regretfully. "That guy just can't make up his mind, can he?"

Lila brought a spoonful of million-dollar-mocha ice cream and whipped cream delicately to her mouth. "Robby, did you have any idea Jeremy was so fickle? What's his deal?"

"I have no idea," Robby said, shaking his head. "All Jeremy's told me is pretty much the same as what Jessica has told you—that he broke off the wedding with Sue because he fell in love with Jessica."

"But is this his pattern?" Lila persisted. "Does he always fool around with other women when he's dating someone?"

"Honestly, Lila, I have no idea," said Robby, spreading his hands out wide. "I've only been friends with Jeremy since I met him at the beach during that volleyball game a few months ago."

Suddenly something clicked in Lila's head. "You became friends with Jeremy when he first arrived in Sweet Valley?"

"Uh-huh." Robby nodded, spooning a scoop of vanilla ice cream into his mouth.

"And how long did you know him before we met you on the beach?" Lila asked.

"Oh, I don't know, about a week, I guess," said Robby.

Lila calculated quickly, her mind whirring with ideas. "So that means that Jeremy had been in Sweet Valley for at least two weeks before he showed up at the Wakefields'."

"Lila, what are you getting at?" Robby asked, a perplexed expression on his face.

"Well, what was he doing here during that time?" Lila said. She brought her head close to Robby's. "Maybe he had some *other* woman in his life then," she concluded.

"I don't know, Lila. I think you're letting your imagination run away with you. Jeremy's not some kind of shark preying the waters of Sweet Valley, California." He stopped to think for a moment. "Actually, when I first met Jeremy, he said he had some business to tend to here."

"Aha!" said Lila, raising her index finger in the air. "What kind of business?"

"I don't know, Lila," said Robby. "But I doubt it was girls."

"Well, Jessica's better off without him," Lila said, shrugging her shoulders dismissively. "He's too old for her anyway."

Robby put on a mock hurt expression. "You mean you don't like older guys?" he asked, taking her hand tenderly.

"Only a couple years older," she said, smiling up at her handsome boyfriend. Robby was eighteen but had decided to put off college for a year in order to devote himself to his art. Lila ruffled Robby's mass of thick black hair and brought his face toward her. They leaned in together for a tender kiss. Lila could taste the sweet flavor of ice cream on Robby's lips. "Umm," she said as they drew back.

"Better than ice cream," Robby agreed, laughing.

"So how are your classes going, Mr. Wall Street?" Lila asked, changing the subject to happier matters. She had enrolled Robby in a business course at Sweet Valley University as a surprise, a surprise that had gone over like a lead bomb. Robby had been furious at her for not consulting him first and had refused even to see if he liked the course. But eventually he had adjusted to the idea, surprising both of them by finding the class to be both useful and interesting. And he had decided to enroll in an art course as well.

"They're going great, Lila," Robby said happily. "My business course is almost over. We have the final next week. And—you'll be happy to know—we've begun painting still lifes in my art class."

"Oh, really," Lila said, feigning apathy. Even though she wouldn't let Robby know it, Lila was actually thrilled that the subject matter in his art class had changed. When she had first found out that Robby was taking a life-drawing class, with male and female nude models, she had been out of her mind with jealousy and had broken up with him. She had eventually realized that he wasn't doing anything wrong, but she still didn't like it.

"I painted a still life of a bowl of fruit last week that turned out pretty well," said Robby. He smiled modestly. "I think I might even be able to show it in my exhibit."

"Robby, just think! Your exhibit is just a few weeks away!" Lila said excitedly. A local gallery in downtown Sweet Valley had agreed to show Robby's paintings in an exhibit of local artists.

"I know. I can't believe it," Robby said. "I sent out all the invitations last night. This will be the first time I've ever publicly displayed my art." His entire face lit up as he talked about the upcoming event.

"Have you chosen all your paintings yet?" asked Lila.

"Well, I haven't gotten the whole collection together yet," Robby said, his bright-blue eyes shining with excitement. "But I have decided to display one portrait prominently."

"Which portrait?" Lila asked.

"The one of you, of course," Robby responded.

Lila smiled sweetly, but an evil idea popped into

her mind. Even though she had tried to adjust to the idea of Robby's art class, the thought of his looking at naked women made her crazy. Maybe he could use a taste of his own medicine, she thought, smiling to herself.

"Hey, Robby, I showed the portrait you did of me to one of my father's friends. His name is Umberto d'Allesandro and he's an artist," she began, allowing a shy smile to cross her face.

"And did he like it?" Robby asked.

"He loved it!" she breathed. "He thinks I have a really special quality. And he said he'd like to do some more paintings of me."

"Lila, that's terrific!" Robby exclaimed. "You *are* my best model." He ran a finger along the outline of her well-defined cheekbone.

"He liked the portrait, but he wants to do some full-body paintings as well," Lila said flippantly.

Robby's body tensed. "Full-body paintings? What do you mean?"

"You know, some full-length nudes. Like in your class," Lila said, her tone nonchalant.

"What?" Robby roared, choking on his soda. "You're going to pose nude?"

"Sure, why not?" Lila responded lightly. "I mean, it's art and everything."

"But, Lila, you—you can't do that," Robby sputtered.

"Why not? I mean, I don't know if I would have considered it before I met you. But like you said, it's all very professional." She sat back and crossed her legs elegantly. "After all, Leonardo da Vinci did it," she said, using one of his old arguments on him.

"It's not the same thing!" Robby's blue eyes were dark with rage, his whole body shaking. "Da Vinci painted the portraits—he didn't *pose* for them. Lila, this is entirely unacceptable. I will not have you sitting naked for hours in front of some man while he studies your body."

"But, Robby, I thought you said it's not like that," said Lila sweetly. "You said it's all very proper, very professional."

"That was different," Robby said.

"Well, I don't think it's any different at all," said Lila pointedly.

"You can do whatever you like, Lila," shouted Robby, standing up abruptly and pulling out his wallet. "But no girlfriend of mine is going to pose naked for paintings!" He threw a handful of bills on the table and stalked to the door.

Lila jumped up. "Robby!" she called after him. "Let me explain!" But Robby had stormed out of the restaurant without a backward glance.

"Darnit!" Lila exclaimed, falling back into her seat. She sighed and spooned the last bit of ice cream out of her sundae dish. She had gone too far again. When would she ever learn?

Elizabeth shivered and wrapped her arms around her body, the tense atmosphere of the normally relaxed household making her feel anxious. It was five P.M., the appointed time for the kidnapper's call. Everybody was gathered together in the living room, staring at the phone in anticipation. Mr. and Mrs. Wakefield were settled together on the couch, and

Sam was sitting by the phone apparatus, ready to trace the call. Jeremy was slouched in the armchair in the corner, a navy-blue baseball cap pulled low over his eyes. He had returned a few minutes before five, a grim expression on his face. Jessica sat on the floor next to him, holding his hand.

Elizabeth wondered what news the call would bring. Her nerves felt raw and stretched from the prolonged strain. *What if the kidnapper says they've done something to Sue?* thought Elizabeth. *What if she's hurt, or worse? Or what if he wants me and Jessica next?*

Suddenly the phone jangled and everybody jumped.

"And they say a watched phone never rings," whispered Jessica to Elizabeth as Ned lifted the receiver off the hook. Elizabeth shook her head, amazed that Jessica could be so flippant at a time like this.

A sinister male voice came across the line. "I see you've disobeyed me," it began slowly. It was the same muffled, menacing voice.

"It's a recording," said the detective, pressing a few buttons on the contraption near the phone. Elizabeth noticed her brow furrow. Sam looked at Jeremy quickly and jotted something down on her yellow legal pad.

"I told you not to go to the authorities," said the voice in an ominous tone. Elizabeth shivered and looked around, feeling as if they were being watched. How did the kidnapper know that they'd hired a detective? "And because you haven't cooperated, you're going to have to pay the price. You'll have to add a hundred thousand dollars to the original sum," continued the voice, "or little Sue's a goner."

"Huh!" Jessica exclaimed, sucking in her breath involuntarily.

"Jessica, shush!" said Mrs. Wakefield, her voice abnormally sharp.

"Please," said the detective calmly, holding up a hand for silence.

"I've set the drop-off for Tuesday night at seven o'clock sharp," continued the muffled voice. Both Sam and Elizabeth hastily scribbled down the information. "Did you get that?" the voice repeated. Elizabeth jumped and looked up from her book. It was as if the voice were watching their every move. "Tomorrow night at seven. At the Glen's Grove gas station off Route Forty-four."

"That's by the cabin!" Elizabeth exclaimed, quickly recording the information in her spiral notebook.

Mrs. Wakefield waved her hand at Elizabeth to be quiet and leaned in to hear as the voice continued. "I want the two girls to do the drop," finished the voice, "and I'm warning you. Leave the detective out of it, or you won't see Sue again."

Dead silence followed the call. Everybody looked at Sam for guidance. She was busy working with the radio transmitter, which was connected to the tracing system in her L.A. office.

"Sam?" asked Ned Wakefield, his voice inquiring.

"We're going to trace the kidnapper to the source," Sam explained calmly. "And then we'll nab him before any of this can be set in motion." She pressed a few buttons and peered at a small readout screen. There was a short beep, and a message flashed forth on the tiny screen. "Source unavailable," read Sam aloud. "What the—?" she muttered under her breath, repeating the procedure. The same message blinked on the screen. "It's a cellular phone," she said finally, "the kidnapper's dream. It's impossible to trace a call from a cellular phone."

Elizabeth could feel Jessica's eyes boring into hers. She turned to find her sister giving her an "I told you so" look. Elizabeth rolled her eyes and looked away.

"I don't want to frighten you," said Sam, "but I'm concerned about the kidnapper's knowledge that I've been put on the case."

"Girls, you haven't said anything about this to your friends, have you?" Mrs. Wakefield asked, looking pointedly at Jessica.

"Of course not!" Jessica responded indignantly. "We haven't talked to a soul, and we've been cooped up in this house alone all day."

"Well, either somebody is watching the house or the place has been bugged," said Sam. Elizabeth shuddered. She pictured the kidnapper hiding out in the closet in her room, or concealed under her bed while she slept. "I'm just going to do a quick inspection of the house."

"I think I'll put on some hot water," said Elizabeth after Sam had left, jumping up and running to the kitchen. Her mind was spinning. The kidnapper wanted more money, Sam couldn't trace the call, and now it looked as if the house was bugged. Elizabeth forced herself to take long, deep breaths as she prepared a pot of chamomile tea. *Maybe some herbal tea will calm us all,* she thought to herself as she returned to the living room with a tray full of cups and saucers.

"Nothing," Sam said, returning to the room as Elizabeth set down the tray. "I checked all the possible sites. Phones, doorways, window latches. The place is sealed tight. I'd advise that you dead-bolt the locks and draw all the curtains this evening," she suggested.

Mrs. Wakefield got up and looked out the windows of the living room. She shivered and drew the curtains quickly.

"Well, it looks as if there's nothing to do for the moment but wait," said Ned, standing up.

"But, Dad," Elizabeth protested, taking a sip of tea, "we can't just sit here. We've got to do something!"

"I know it's tough, Liz," said Mr. Wakefield sympathetically, "but we can't act rashly. This is a very delicate case, and Sam's got a lot of investigative work to do before we can take action."

"Mr. Wakefield's right," agreed Jeremy, jumping up and pacing the room like a caged animal. "We've got to be extremely prudent in this situation. We can't take any drastic measures—for Sue's sake."

"Well, I'm going to go back to my L.A. office tonight to follow up on some leads," said Sam, standing up. "I'll be back in the morning. Until then we're all going to have to sit tight."

Elizabeth bit her lip but didn't say anything. She knew they couldn't do anything hasty. As if they could do anything at all! They had no idea who the kidnapper was, where he was calling from, or where Sue was being held captive.

"And I repeat my warning about utter secrecy regarding this case," said Sam in a somber voice. "Any transgression on your parts could jeopardize Sue's life." She looked around as everyone nodded solemnly.

Suddenly the phone rang again. They all jumped and stared at it as if it were the enemy. "I've just about had enough of this," Ned said in an angry tone as he reached for the phone. "What do you want now?" he asked, his voice harsh. He listened for a moment. "Oh," he said, and handed the phone to Jessica. "It's for you."

"Hello?" Jessica said, taking the receiver from her father's outstretched hand.

"Well, that was quite a greeting," said Lila, her voice wry.

"It's just Lila," Jessica mouthed to her family, picking up the phone and sitting down in the armchair with it. She placed the phone in her lap and held the receiver to her ear.

"Has your father been spending too many hours at the office?" Lila went on.

"Uh, yeah, I think he's under a bit of strain," said Jessica. "Sorry about that. He was expecting someone else."

"Like a tax collector?" asked Lila.

"Something like that," said Jessica. She changed the subject quickly. "So what's up, Li? Any gossip?"

Lila's voice burst forth on the line. "Jessica, you

111

won't believe what I've done!" she exclaimed.

"Oh, no," responded Jessica. "Not another Robby fiasco."

Lila quickly filled Jessica in on the events of her meeting with Robby at Casey's.

"Well, he got what he deserved," said Jessica after Lila had finished recounting her tale. "You gave him a taste of his own medicine."

"But now I've ruined everything again!" Lila wailed.

"Don't worry, Lila," Jessica said in a comforting voice. "He'll understand. Just call him and explain it to him. Tell him it was just a joke and that you never thought he'd react so strongly."

"I guess you're right. In any case, it was pretty satisfying to turn the tables on him," she said in a brighter tone. "Oh, Jess, you should have seen his face." Lila giggled into the phone. "He looked like he was about to explode!"

Jessica laughed with her. "Ah, the sweet taste of revenge!" she said.

"Hey, why weren't you in school today?" Lila asked.

Jessica hesitated momentarily. She was desperate to give Lila the news. She took the phone into the corner of the room and looked around surreptitiously. Everybody was talking animatedly on the other side of the room.

Jessica turned her back to the others and spoke softly into the phone. "Lila, you won't believe what's going on here!" she whispered.

"What?" Lila asked.

"I can't tell you now," Jessica said, twisting her head and looking over at the detective nervously.

"Jess!" Lila exclaimed. "You have to tell me!"

Jessica didn't need much convincing. "OK, but you can't tell anyone," she said in a hushed tone. "Promise?"

"Yes, yes, of course I promise," Lila answered, sounding exasperated. "Now, why weren't you in school today?" she demanded.

Jessica covered the mouthpiece with her hand as she spoke. "We're staying home because Sue's been kidnapped. She's being held hostage."

"You're what?" Lila repeated. "Jessica, I can barely hear you! Are you all right?"

"Listen, I've gotta go," Jessica said suddenly as she noticed her father and the detective approaching as they walked to the door.

Lila sat on the edge of her bed, staring at the receiver of her powder-blue Princess phone. What had Jessica been trying to say? She tried to piece together what she had heard. "We've . . . kidnapped . . . an ostrich." An ostrich? They kidnapped an ostrich?

Lila puzzled out the words again, trying to make sense of them. "An ostrich—an ostrich," Lila repeated out loud. "A hostage! Held hostage!" Suddenly Jessica's words came back to her. "We're . . . kidnapped . . . held hostage." That's it! The Wakefields were being held hostage! So that's why Mrs. Wakefield had been so jumpy this morning. And that's why Mr. Wakefield had been so harsh on the phone— they must be in trouble, in big trouble.

Lila stared at the phone in distress, wondering what to do. She wished she could tell her father, but he was away on business in London. And her mother was with him for the week as well. Lila thought for a moment and then picked up the phone.

Chapter 10

Todd was propped up on his back on his bed Monday evening, listlessly throwing a foam ball into the hoop attached to his dresser drawer. He was wondering why Elizabeth hadn't been in school that day. And he was wondering why she sounded so strange on the phone when he called her from school. Maybe she was grounded, he thought to himself. Grounded from school? What was he thinking?

Suddenly the ringing of the phone cut into his thoughts. *Elizabeth!* he thought, and swooped up the receiver.

"Hi, Todd, it's Lila."

"Oh, hi, Lila," Todd said, trying to keep the disappointment out of his voice. Why in the world was Lila Fowler calling him? Lila had never particularly acted as if she liked him, and the feeling was mutual.

"Todd, the Wakefields are being held hostage!"

Lila exclaimed, skipping all pleasantries. Her voice was urgent.

"Lila, what in the world are you talking about?" Todd said, falling onto his back on the bed. He cradled the receiver in the crook of his neck and threw the ball in the air with one hand.

"The Wakefields are being held hostage!" Lila repeated.

"The Wakefields are being held hostage?" Todd scoffed. "Lila, I think you've been watching way too much TV."

"Todd, I am telling you, Jessica's family is in danger!" Lila insisted. Todd could hear the frustration in her voice.

"OK, Lila, calm down," Todd said, forcing a more tolerant note to his voice. "What makes you think that an entire family is being held hostage in their own home?"

"I just called Jessica on the phone. She could barely talk, but she risked her life and managed to whisper what's going on," Lila explained.

Todd was losing patience. He didn't know what Jessica was up to, but he had no tolerance for it at the moment. "Lila, I'm sure she's just playing a little trick on you. Or maybe you misunderstood what she was saying."

"Todd, it's true, I'm sure of it," Lila insisted. "There's more. . . ." Todd listened as Lila explained about Mrs. Wakefield's bizarre behavior earlier that morning and Mr. Wakefield's uncommonly gruff attitude on the phone.

Todd was beginning to feel worried in spite of

himself. It was possible that the Wakefields were just strung out because of everything that had been going on with Jessica and Sue and Jeremy. But Elizabeth *had* sounded extremely strange on the phone. And Todd *had* had a feeling all day that something was wrong. The story was outlandish, but, still—what if it was true? Suddenly Todd was afraid.

"Lila, I'm going to call Liz," Todd determined, sitting up suddenly.

"No, Todd, you can't!" Lila insisted. "You might provoke the kidnapper. Maybe we should call the police."

"I don't know," Todd said, considering the option. "I don't think the police would come without any evidence. And they probably wouldn't believe us, anyway."

"Well, we've got to do something," Lila said.

Todd was silent for a moment, thinking. "Lila, why don't we check it out for ourselves?" he suggested. "That way we'll know what to do next."

"OK," Lila agreed. "We'll see for ourselves. I'll get Robby and pick you up in fifteen minutes."

Five minutes later Lila pulled her lime-green Triumph to a halt in front of the cottage Robby lived in with his father. She smoothed down her hair and took a deep breath. She had completely forgotten about her fight with Robby when she was talking to Todd. But she needed Robby's help now. Lila and Todd needed somebody to keep watch in the car while they scouted the lawns. And Robby was the only person Lila could trust.

Lila took a deep breath and marched up to the

cottage door. She thumped the brass knocker three times insistently.

Robby's father answered the door. "Oh, hi, Lila," he said, his deeply lined face crinkling into a friendly smile. "Looking for Robby?"

Lila nodded her head impatiently.

"Robby!" Mr. Goodman called up the stairs. "You've got a visitor!"

A few moments later Robby's face appeared at the banister. Lila smoothed down her shirt nervously. "Lila?" Robby asked, his voice incredulous. "What a surprise."

"I know," Lila responded impatiently. "We've gotta go," she said, her voice urgent. "I'll explain in the car. C'mon!"

"Robby, I want to explain, I—" Lila began as soon as they were safely on the road.

"Lila, I'm sorry, I—" Robby said at the same time.

They both laughed uncomfortably. "Let me start," Robby said, shifting in the seat and turning to face her. "Lila, I'm sorry about what I said earlier. I was wrong. You have the right to do anything you want," he said. "Even if that thing is, um, posing nude." He grimaced a little at the thought.

Lila whipped around to face him. His expression was completely sincere. "Really?" Lila asked, turning her attention back to the road. She was stunned at his sudden about-face.

"Really," said Robby, reaching over to brush a strand of hair off Lila's cheek. "There's nothing wrong with my taking a life-drawing class or with your posing as an artist's model. But I guess I understand now why it bothered you. I can see why my class has been hard for you."

Lila swallowed, feeling grateful. Maybe she could just tell him that she had changed her mind about being a model, she thought to herself. But she knew she had to tell him the truth. Lila took a deep breath and plunged ahead. "Uh, Robby," Lila said, swallowing hard, "actually, I'm not really planning to pose as a nude model."

"You're not?" Robby asked, his eyes lighting up. "All right!" He addressed an imaginary audience. "Ladies and gentlemen, she's giving up her modeling career!" He turned to Lila. "Wild applause from the audience," he said.

Lila couldn't help smiling. "And I never was planning to do it, anyway," she went on. "My father *does* have an artist friend named Umberto. But he doesn't want to paint me. He lives in San Francisco. And I never showed him the portrait."

"What?" Robby exclaimed. "You made it all up?"

Lila nodded her head sheepishly.

"Because you wanted to get back at me—?" Robby guessed.

Lila shook her head. "It wasn't so much that I wanted revenge. It was more that I just wanted you to understand what it was like for me," she explained. She turned imploring eyes on him. "Robby, I'm sorry."

"I can't believe it!" Robby exclaimed. "Foiled again! Lila Fowler, you are certainly a handful!"

Lila smiled to herself. She *was* a handful. And

Robby was just going to have to get used to it.

Lila made a sharp turn onto Country Club Drive and pulled the car to a screeching halt in front of the Wilkinses' brick mansion. She honked the horn hard.

"Lila?" Robby said, turning to look at her.

"Yes?" she asked as Todd came running out of the house, dressed in black jeans and a black T-shirt.

"What are we doing here?" Robby asked.

"Oh, I almost forgot. The Wakefields have been kidnapped," Lila said.

"The house looks deserted," said Todd, twisting around uncomfortably as they rounded the corner on Calico Drive. He and Robby were crammed together in the front seat of Lila's two-seater car.

"It's completely dark," Lila breathed, taking in the somber Wakefield home down the street. She cut the headlights and coasted slowly down the block. "It's as if the place has been abandoned."

"The shades are probably just drawn," surmised Robby. "Kidnappers don't usually invite the neighbors in."

"Lila, you should probably park in front of the neighbor's house," Todd suggested. Lila pulled the car in close to the curb and wrenched up the parking brake.

"OK, this is it," said Lila, jumping out of the car lightly. Todd and Robby clambered out quickly after her. Todd massaged his cramped legs and Robby stretched his arms over his head. Lila shivered and pulled her jacket closer around her. The night was unseasonably cool and misty.

Lila handed the ignition keys to Robby. He took them from her and pulled her in for a quick hug. "Be careful," he warned them both. "Any sign of trouble, run. I'll be ready and waiting."

"And, Robby, remember, if you hear a whistle, call the police—on the car phone," Lila said. Robby nodded, looking grim.

"Lila, let's go," urged Todd.

Robby settled into the driver's seat and gave them a thumbs-up signal. Todd and Lila returned the gesture and made their way quickly across the lawn of the neighbor's house. The Wakefield home was still shrouded in darkness, giving off the impression of a haunted house. Todd fought the urge to run to the front door and barge in. He had an overwhelming desire to see Elizabeth's face. He just wanted to see that she was OK and to hold her in his arms.

"Stay low and hurry," warned Todd when they reached the front yard of the Wakefield house. They sneaked along the lawn until they reached the side of the house. "Get down!" Todd barked, noticing a shaft of light coming through a bedroom window on the second floor in the front of the house. He crouched down on the grass, pulling Lila down with him. The light was coming from Elizabeth's room. Was she in there? Todd wondered to himself. Was she hurt?

Todd's heart began to pound. They had to find a way to see into the house. Todd thought quickly. He knew there was a small decorative window in the kitchen that didn't have a curtain. That was probably their best chance. "Let's try the kitchen," he suggested.

"OK," Lila agreed, rolling back on her heels to get

up. Todd reached out a hand and stopped her. "Lila, we're going to have to shimmy across the lawn," Todd said. He dived onto the grass and lay flat on his stomach, propping himself up with his elbows.

Lila lifted a perfectly arched eyebrow and looked down at Todd's prone figure. "Excuse me?" she asked.

"We can't just walk across the lawn! We can't risk being seen through a curtain in the family room," Todd hissed. "Now, c'mon," he said, losing patience.

Lila took a deep breath and dropped to her knees. She carefully adopted the position Todd had assumed. "Oh, gross!" she exclaimed as her body made contact with the damp, hard ground. She watched with distaste as Todd began slithering across the lawn like a snake, padding along on his hands and elbows.

Lila sighed and wriggled along after him, slowly inching across the wet grass on her stomach. "I'm ruining my new jacket," Lila complained when she reached him. She looked over her tapered black leather jacket with concern.

Todd rolled his eyes and continued slithering along the grass. Lila stopped and rolled back on her heels to inspect the sleeves of her jacket. "I think I'm getting grass stains on this," she said in dismay.

Todd looked back at her in exasperation. "Lila, would you c'mon?" he said. She sighed and lay back down in the grass, shimmying to his side by the fence surrounding the patio. They inched carefully around the backyard until they reached the opposite side of the house.

"Lila, look!" Todd said excitedly, pointing to the tiny square kitchen window visible from the side of the house. "I'm going to take a look. Stand guard, OK?"

Lila flattened her body against the side of the house, looking carefully both ways for any signs of trouble. Todd held on to the windowsill and hoisted himself high enough to look into the kitchen window. The usually bright and gay Wakefield kitchen was gray and foreboding, covered in shadows. Todd shivered and dropped down.

"They're not there," he whispered to Lila. "Let's try the family room." Todd fought a moment of panic, imagining the entire family tied up and the kidnapper torturing Elizabeth. He pictured a gruff man standing above her with a gleaming kitchen knife, drawing small patterns in the air around her head while she stared at the knife, her eyes bulging in fear.

They inched around behind the house until they got to the side window of the family room. Todd jumped, springing as high as his six-foot frame would allow. He was a full foot short. He tried again but couldn't come near it. "It's too high," Todd said, frustrated.

"Todd, put me on your shoulders," Lila whispered. Todd knelt down in the wet grass and allowed Lila to climb onto his shoulders. He steadied her ankles with his hands and stood up slowly.

Lila peered into the window. Jessica and Elizabeth were huddled together on the sofa, looking miserable. Mrs. Wakefield was sitting in an armchair with her head in her hands, a resigned look on her face. Mr. Wakefield was sitting on the stone ledge in front of the fireplace, a look of fierce determination creasing his brow.

"They're all there!" exclaimed Lila. Todd heaved his shoulders in relief, almost toppling Lila in the process. "Todd!" she hissed, grabbing at the shingles on the house to steady herself. She looked back into the family room. Suddenly a chill ran down her spine as she noticed a sinister form standing in the shadows at the far end of the room. He was about six feet tall and wearing a baseball cap. "He's there!" Lila hissed. "The kidnapper's there!" She peered through the windowpane to get a better look, but the baseball cap shielded his face from her view.

Suddenly the form began moving toward the window. "Todd! Quick! Let me down!" Lila said. "He's coming!"

Todd held firmly on to Lila's ankles and knelt. Lila dropped to the ground gracefully.

"C'mon, let's go!" she urged. They sprinted across the back lawn and through the grass until they reached Lila's car.

Robby turned over the engine as he saw them arriving. They dived into the car, and Robby quickly backed around the corner.

"Robby, he's there! The kidnapper's there with the Wakefields!" Lila exclaimed.

"Did you see everybody?" Todd asked anxiously. "Was Liz OK?"

"They were all there, and they were all fine," answered Lila, breathing heavily. "But the kidnapper was stalking around the room, and they all looked miserable."

"What did he look like?" asked Robby.

"I couldn't make him out very well," Lila answered. "But he was big and looked dangerous."

Todd's stomach knotted in fear. Elizabeth was in danger. He had to do something. "Robby, let's go in there," Todd said suddenly, grabbing the door handle. "We'll rush the place."

"Todd, you can't," Lila said, putting a hand on his arm to stop him. "It's too dangerous."

"Robby and I are strong. We can take on one man, no problem," Todd insisted. "And we're not afraid, right, Robby?"

"Todd, he'll have a weapon," Lila argued. "Courage is worthless in the face of a gun. All you'd accomplish is to get yourselves killed. And probably the Wakefields as well."

"Todd, Lila's right," Robby agreed. "We can't act rashly. We'd probably just end up locked in the house with them." Todd considered the possibility. At least he'd be by Elizabeth's side. But Robby was right. He couldn't help her if he just got held up inside the house as well.

"I think we should call the police," Lila said.

"No, that would endanger the family even more," Todd said. "The police would just surround the place. And anything could happen inside." Todd thought back to all the mystery movies he had seen in which the police surround a house and the kidnapper comes out with a hostage in front of him as protection. Todd shivered, imagining Elizabeth being held by a man with a gun as the police shout through megaphones, "Come out! Come out! The house is surrounded!"

"Well, we've got to do something," Robby said, revving the motor and backing down the street.

"We need a plan," agreed Todd, his dark-brown eyes clouded with worry.

"This way!" Todd said as he spotted a vacant booth in the back of the Dairi Burger. The noisy diner wasn't exactly private, but it was the closest place around. Lila, Todd, and Robby threaded their way carefully through the crowded restaurant, averting their eyes to avoid their friends.

Todd gazed around the tightly packed room as they squeezed into the corner booth. The popular teen hangout was hopping as usual, crowded with young people talking animatedly and happily devouring burgers and shakes. Winston and Maria were sitting with a group of friends in a big booth in front, laughing uproariously at a joke someone had made. Enid Rollins and her boyfriend Hugh were holding hands across a small wooden table, engrossed in what seemed to be an intimate conversation. Todd shook his head. It was unreal. All their friends were leading normal lives while Elizabeth and her family were being held hostage by some madman.

"Can I help you?" asked the waitress in a friendly voice, poised above them with a notepad in her hand. They placed their orders quickly. Lila and Robby ordered fries and shakes, but Todd just asked for water. The thought of food made him nauseous.

Todd turned to the others as soon as the waitress was out of earshot. "We've got to figure out a way to get into the house," he declared.

"And we've got to do it secretly," added Robby, "so we can unarm the kidnapper without endangering the Wakefields."

"What if we break into the kitchen window?" suggested Todd. "Then Robby and I can sneak up on the kidnapper and attack him from behind."

"Todd, that is such a juvenile idea," said Lila, her voice dripping with disdain. "We can't just run in and jump on the guy. It's too risky," she said. She looked down her nose at him, an imperial expression on her patrician face.

Todd clenched his fists into balls. "Well, then, Lila, what would you suggest?" A muscle twitched involuntarily in his cheek. Todd was getting tired of Lila's prima donna attitude. Lila just didn't want to get her clothes dirty in a skirmish.

"Well, if you knew anything at all about the world of subterfuge," said Lila in a haughty tone, "then you would know that the best way to do something secretly is to do it out in the open."

Todd stared at her. "What in the world are you talking about?" he asked.

"Lila's right!" Robby said, jumping on the idea. "We've got to walk right up to the front door. We've got to make the kidnapper let us in."

"You mean, you want to come as the police or something?" Todd asked.

"No, no, not as the police," said Lila. "But in disguise. In a disguise that will make the kidnapper just open the door and invite us in."

"You mean, like if we pretended we were plumbers or something?" Todd asked.

Lila nodded. "Right. But somehow a plumber is not exactly what I had in mind," she said.

"How about if we came as firemen?" suggested Robby. "We could burst in the door saying there was a fire in the basement."

"And then we could spray the kidnapper with a fire extinguisher," said Todd excitedly.

"I don't know," said Lila, shaking her head. "We'd need uniforms. Not to mention a fire truck."

"Yeah, and fire trucks are municipal property," said Todd. "I don't know how we'd get our hands on one."

"OK, let's think," said Lila. "Now, who has access to a house? The fire department, plumbers, sanitation workers—"

Todd joined in. "The telephone company, electrical workers—"

"Electrical workers! That's it!" Robby exclaimed, his eyes lighting up with excitement.

Just then the waitress appeared and set down their food.

"Electrical workers?" Lila asked as soon as she was gone. She picked up a fry and dredged it in ketchup.

"My cousin Sidney works at Sweet Valley Power," Robby said, speaking quickly. "He's a vice president in the corporate office. He could get us SVP worker uniforms and maybe a truck."

"It's perfect!" Lila breathed. "We can say the electricity has gone out and—"

"No, that wouldn't work" Todd interrupted her, shaking his head. "They'll know the electricity's working." He thought for a moment. "But we could claim that there has been a water-main break on the Wakefields' block and that the electrical wiring of the neighborhood has been affected."

"Great!" said Robby. "So then we would need to get into the basement in order to check the breaker box. We'd have to make sure there wouldn't be a short when they adjusted the power." He took a gulp of his chocolate shake. "And it's a town ordinance that all residents have to give electrical workers access to the breaker boxes in an emergency."

"And then the kidnapper would have to hide his gun while we're in the house," Lila added. "So that would be the perfect time to get him."

"Right!" said Todd. Then his face fell. "But how? How will we get him?"

"With flame-retardant spray, that's how," said Robby. "That's what they use at SVP in case of an electrical fire. It's the same as a fire extinguisher."

"OK, so here's the plan," said Todd, taking charge. He looked around quickly, making sure no one was listening. Robby and Lila leaned in close to hear. "Once we're inside, I'll go down into the basement to check the box, and you two will stand by the family, keeping an eye on the kidnapper," Todd said in a low voice. "Then I'll turn off the breaker box."

"And the lights!" put in Robby, impressed with the idea.

"Exactly," said Todd. "And in the ensuing confusion Lila will spray the kidnapper. And Robby will be standing by his side in case force is needed."

Lila swallowed hard. "Did you say you want me to

spray the kidnapper?" she asked, her smooth brow wrinkling at the thought.

"What's wrong, Fowler?" Todd challenged. "Are you afraid to get your clothes dirty?"

"Of course not," Lila said indignantly. "I just wanted to make sure."

"OK, let's go!" Todd said, springing out of his chair. "Let's go call Sidney."

"Whoa, whoa, slow down," Robby said. "We can't do anything until the morning."

"But we've got to go into action immediately," insisted Todd. "Elizabeth's family is in danger!"

"Todd, we might be able to get the uniforms from the plant tonight, but we wouldn't be able to get a truck. We'll have to check one out during the day," Robby explained. "Todd, buddy, believe me, patience will serve us in the end. If we don't want to endanger the Wakefields, we have to plan this out to perfection," said Robby.

Todd nodded slowly. "I guess you're right," he said, sitting down reluctantly. He glanced at his watch. Nine o'clock. He studied the second hand as it wound slowly around the Roman face. How would he ever make it through the night?

Chapter 11

Elizabeth paced back and forth in the living room on Tuesday morning, flipping through the pages of her notebook. The sound of the pages turning seemed to fill the entire room. Even though it was midmorning, the normally lively house was dark and eerily quiet. Jessica was still sleeping, and Mr. and Mrs. Wakefield were holding a private conference with Sam in the study.

Elizabeth shivered as she thought of the day to come. Today was the drop-off day. *D day*, Elizabeth thought to herself wryly. And she and Jessica were the decoys. Her tongue went dry as she thought of it. They simply had to prevent the drop-off from occurring, Elizabeth thought with determination. She puzzled through her notes again. There had to be a clue to the mystery in them somewhere. She read the last lines aloud. *Ransom amount equals inheritance. Kidnapping occurs on day Sue to receive inheritance*. Who else knew of the inheritance? Who would want to harm Sue?

The sounds of her parents' muffled voices drifted toward her from the study. Elizabeth wondered what Sam had discovered at the office. Had she come up with any possible suspects? Had she uncovered any information on Phil Schmitt? Elizabeth had asked to be included in the conference, but Sam had insisted on privacy.

Elizabeth sighed in frustration. How could she be of help if she didn't have any information? She flipped through the pages of her notebook again and then threw it onto an armchair in frustration. Her journal was worthless. She glanced down the hall to her father's study. She simply had to know what was going on in there if she was going to help Sue. After all, a good reporter had to have all the facts, right?

Elizabeth quickly retrieved her book and tip-toed down the hall. She held her breath as she approached the solid oak door and pressed her ear up against it.

". . . and I went through all the police files of the greater southern California area as well," Sam was saying. "No case matches this one."

"What about that kidnapping last summer in Santa Monica? Of the little Collins girl?" Mrs. Wakefield asked.

"That was orchestrated by a drug ring," said Sam. She lowered her voice, and Elizabeth strained to hear. "Frankly, Alice," said Sam, "I don't think this is

132

the right route to take. We're not dealing with a professional abductor here. Or a hired hand. The case is too personal. The kidnapper has access to too much insider information."

"Sam's right," put in Mr. Wakefield. "We're talking about somebody who is intimately acquainted with the Gibbons family affairs."

Elizabeth shuddered at her father's words. Somehow the idea of the kidnapper being personally related to Sue made him more menacing than some anonymous criminal. Elizabeth wondered if the kidnapper was someone she knew.

"Did you get any information on Sue's stepfather?" asked Mrs. Wakefield.

"I ran a complete background check on Phil Schmitt," said Sam. "So far he looks completely clean. I'll give you what I've got. Let's see—" Elizabeth could hear the sound of pages turning. "Phil Schmitt, forty-five years old," recited Sam. "Grew up in Greenwich, Connecticut. Comes from old money. Runs a successful ad agency in Manhattan." Elizabeth frantically recorded the information in her journal as Sam spoke. "Married previously and divorced, no kids. Happily remarried for eight years. Grieving since the loss of his second wife . . ." Sam's voice trailed off.

Elizabeth listened closely but couldn't make out any more. The room was silent. Had they heard the sounds of her pen scratching across the page? She held her breath and waited, her heart pounding in her chest.

". . . still doesn't make sense. After all, why

wouldn't she leave the money to him instead of me?" her mother was saying, her voice muffled. Elizabeth breathed a sigh of relief as the conversation resumed. Mrs. Wakefield must have taken a chair in the back of the study.

"I don't think that's so odd," said Sam. "After all, Phil Schmitt is independently wealthy. I imagine Nancy wanted the inheritance in the hands of somebody impartial. The situation would have put Phil in a difficult position—torn between his wife and his stepdaughter."

"So what do you suggest, Sam?" asked Mr. Wakefield. His voice sounded deadly serious.

"I'm afraid we're going to have to go through with the drop," said the detective.

But we can't do that! Elizabeth wanted to scream. She clapped her hand against her mouth, fighting the urge to barge into the room and protest. She couldn't believe Sam was just going to let the kidnapper get away with it. Maybe Jessica was right after all.

"I was afraid of that," said Mrs. Wakefield.

"It doesn't look like we have any options at this point, does it?" asked Mr. Wakefield.

"Oh, Ned, I'm so torn," said Mrs. Wakefield. The anguish was plain in her mother's voice. "I'd do anything to save Sue, but not at the cost of my daughters' lives."

"Don't worry, Alice," said Sam. "They'll be fully protected. They'll be equipped with bug devices, and I'll be right on their tail." Elizabeth breathed a sigh of relief.

"Now, this is the plan," Sam said, lowering her

voice to a whisper. Elizabeth leaned in closer to the door. She could barely make out her words. "Ned will go out to the bank today and pick up the ransom. Now, about the money . . ."

Elizabeth pressed her ear harder against the door. She couldn't hear a thing. She listened carefully for a few minutes, but Sam's voice remained inaudible. Suddenly she heard the sounds of chairs scraping and footsteps approaching. Elizabeth dashed away from the door and ducked into the kitchen as her parents emerged. She flattened her body against the wall, her heart beating furiously. *What about the money?* she screamed silently in her head.

"Liz?" called her father, poking his head into the kitchen.

"Oh, hi, Dad," said Elizabeth, trying to keep her voice from shaking. She peeled herself from the wall and hopped up on one of the stools, trying to act casual.

"Listen, I'm just running out to the bank," Mr. Wakefield said, his tone nonchalant. "I'll be back soon. But don't hold lunch for me."

"Sure, Dad," said Elizabeth, forcing a weak smile. "See you soon." She leaned back against the counter, her whole body trembling. *As soon as you return with over half a million dollars—that Jessica and I are going to hand over to a deadly kidnapper.*

Sue opened her eyes slowly and tried to rub the sleep out of them, but her hands wouldn't budge. "Jeremy?" she said aloud, looking around the room bewildered. Where was she? Why did she feel as if

135

she couldn't move? *It must be a dream,* Sue thought, closing her eyes tightly and opening them again. Suddenly it all came back to her. Unfortunately, this wasn't a dream. It was a nightmare. Sue was pretending to be kidnapped. And she was alone in a dark attic. Tied up to a wooden chair.

Sue rotated her head slowly around her shoulders, trying to work out the stiffness in her neck. She tensed the muscles in her body in an attempt to stretch them out. Finally she leaned her head back wearily against the chair. Every muscle ached. She could feel her joints screaming in agony, begging to be freed. She wished Jeremy would stop by so she could at least get up and stretch her legs for a minute or two.

Sue sighed, thinking back to her argument with Jeremy the night before. He had brought her a sandwich for dinner, and he had even allowed her to remain untied for half an hour. She had practically begged him to let her stay in his room with him, but he had refused. He had been adamant, saying it was a risk they couldn't take. When she had pushed it, he had mocked her for her weakness and left in a huff. Sue exhaled deeply. The night had been excruciating and endless. She had drifted in and out of sleep, shifting constantly to find a comfortable position. At one point she had even considered toppling the chair over, so she could at least lie down. But that would have been even worse. She would have felt even more panicked pinned to the floor with a chair attached to her.

Sue twisted her head around to get a glimpse of her watch. It was nine o'clock. Jeremy was probably sleeping soundly in his comfortable bed. He would be going over to the Wakefields' soon so he could pass a few romantic hours with Jessica Wakefield. And make a show of his concern for Sue.

What I fool I've been, Sue berated herself. She had been completely taken with Jeremy. She had believed his stories about his total disregard for money. And she had eaten up his professions of love for her. But now she was afraid she was seeing him for what he really was. A greedy young man who was interested in her only for her money.

It's all my fault, Sue realized suddenly. Her mother had tried to warn her all along. She had done everything in her power to prevent this from happening. She had even gone so far as to write her only daughter out of her will to keep her from making a terrible mistake. Sue had no one to blame but herself. Well, Sue determined, she got herself into this situation and she would get herself out. Her jaw set in determination as she made a stiff-resolve. She wasn't going to go through with this plan. Jeremy Randall could do whatever he liked. He could have the money for all she cared. But he was going to have to get it himself. Sue was officially out.

"Todd!" Lila whispered, popping her head into study hall. Todd looked up and saw Lila beckoning to him from the hall. He grabbed his books and slipped quietly out of the classroom.

"How did you get out of French class?" asked Todd in a low voice as they made their way carefully down the hallway.

"Oh, I gave Ms. Dalton a note from my father," Lila explained with a wave of her hand. "They can't check it."

"Good thinking," Todd said, berating himself for his lack of resourcefulness. They had some important errands to do, picking up a disguise for Lila at the costume store and a tool kit at the hardware store. But Todd didn't have a note or a hall pass. If they were stopped, he wouldn't be able to leave the building. Todd looked around furtively, breathing a sigh of relief as he took in the deserted corridor.

"Lila, let's hurry," he said, picking up his pace as they turned the corner. He turned his head toward her, but she was gone. "Lila?" Todd asked, looking around him furiously.

"Chrome Dome Cooper!" Lila hissed from the doorway of the girls' john. She indicated the far end of the hallway with a flick of her head and ducked into the rest room. Todd stopped dead in his tracks. The principal was shuffling down the hall toward him, the fluorescent lights of the ceiling reflecting off his bald head.

Todd continued his route, making his way casually to the water fountain. He pressed down the metal button and slowly drank from the spout. Todd's heart thumped in his chest as the principal walked by. After Chrome Dome had passed, Todd leaned down to tie his shoe, forcing himself to count to ten before he looked back.

Finally Todd glanced down the hall. Mr. Cooper was nowhere in sight. Todd scooted into the girls' rest room to fetch Lila.

His entrance was greeted by a wrenching scream. "Todd!" exclaimed Olivia Davidson when she realized who it was. "What are you doing in here?" Olivia was standing in front of the mirror, a stick of lipstick poised in front of her face.

Lila was seated on the counter, swinging her legs back and forth. She looked up at Todd with an amused smirk.

"Oh, Olivia, I'm so sorry, I thought this was the boys' rest room," stammered Todd, his face flushing. He backed out awkwardly.

"See you, Liv," said Lila. She followed Todd into the hall, unable to contain her laughter.

Todd wasn't amused. "Lila, it isn't funny!" he said, glowering at her. He looked around the hall frantically, panicked that someone had heard Olivia's scream. "Now, c'mon!" he said, grabbing her by the arm. "We've got to make a run for it!" They ran full speed down the hall to the double doors leading to the parking lot.

"Is there a problem in here?" they heard the principal's voice boom as they dashed out the door.

"Let's see—tomatoes, cucumbers, onions," said Mrs. Wakefield, setting down a pile of fresh vegetables on the kitchen counter in front of Elizabeth. She was scurrying around the kitchen in a white apron, preparing lunch.

Elizabeth watched in disbelief as her mother

bustled around the kitchen, acting as if everything were normal. She shook her head and sliced into a tomato.

Mrs. Wakefield took stock of the pile of vegetables laid out on the counter. "We're out of pickles!" she exclaimed. She shook her head regretfully. "Cold cuts with no pickles! Liz, do you think we should have something different?"

"No, Mom, I don't think anybody will miss them," said Elizabeth, forcing herself to exhale. She realized that she had been unconsciously holding her breath. Despite all her mother's attempts at normalcy, the house was fairly crackling with tension. Elizabeth looked up at the wooden clock on the kitchen wall. It seemed to tick audibly as the seconds inched by, bringing them closer and closer to the drop-off time.

"Liz, dear, could you give me the fruit bowl?" Elizabeth jumped at the sound of her mother's voice.

"Oh, sure, Mom," said Elizabeth, handing her mother the large ceramic bowl from the counter. She took a deep breath to calm her frazzled nerves.

"Where's Jess, honey?" asked her mother, filling the bowl with bunches of red and purple grapes.

"She's out by the pool with Jeremy," Elizabeth said, drawing back the blinds and peeking out the glass doors. It was a hot, beautiful day, and Jessica and Jeremy were lying together on chaise lounges in front of the sparkling pool. Elizabeth shook her head in wonder. How could they be sunbathing at a time like this?

"Liz, do you think you could set the table?" asked Mrs. Wakefield, heading for the refrigerator. She grabbed two loaves of bread, a bag of turnips, a head of lettuce, a carton of milk, and a jar of mustard from the refrigerator. Her hands full, she tucked the condiment jar under her arm and steadied the milk carton with her chin. Balancing the stack carefully, she kicked the door shut and began maneuvering her way to the counter.

"Mom!" said Elizabeth when she saw the impending avalanche. "Let me help you!"

"That's all right, I've got it," said Mrs. Wakefield. She stopped at the kitchen counter, allowing the food to tumble out of her arms onto the tabletop. The mustard jar began rolling across the counter. Mrs. Wakefield caught it at the edge and began sorting through the food.

"Mom, why don't you sit down? I'll make the sandwiches," Elizabeth offered, watching her mother with concern. Her obsessive behavior reminded Elizabeth of another unhappy time. Elizabeth had been involved in the accident that had caused the death of Sam Woodruff, Jessica's boyfriend. When Elizabeth had been forced to stand trial for manslaughter, her mother had gone into a state of deep denial. Unable to face the possibility of her daughter's conviction, she had escaped into housework, putting up a front that everything was normal as she obsessively cooked and cleaned.

"Thanks, honey," said Alice, picking up a sponge and running it over the spotless kitchen counter. She grabbed an electric broom from the corner and began running it back and forth on the immaculate Spanish-tiled floor.

"Mom?" Elizabeth said softly, touching her mother's shoulder.

"Yes, dear?" said Mrs. Wakefield, turning to face her. Her blues eyes were troubled and dark with concern. There were deep circles under her eyes, the result of all the stress brought about by the situation with Sue and Jessica.

"Nothing," said Elizabeth, turning back to the food. She was pained to see the anguish in her mother's eyes, but relieved that she was facing reality.

"Mmm," said Jessica, luxuriating in the feel of the hot sun sinking into her body. She stretched like a cat, arching her back and raising her arms above her head. Jessica was wearing a new aqua string bikini that matched the color of her eyes, and she knew she looked stunning.

"Hmm?" Jeremy said, his voice distracted. He didn't turn his head.

Jessica clenched her jaw in frustration. Ever since Sue had disappeared, Jeremy hadn't paid an ounce of attention to her. Here she was, lying next to him in all her splendor, and he didn't even notice. In fact, he didn't even seem to be aware of her presence at all.

"Jeremy?" Jessica said, turning his face toward hers. "Is something the matter? You seem preoccupied."

"Oh, no, nothing's the matter," said Jeremy, leaning his head back and closing his eyes. "I'm just worried about Sue, that's all."

Jessica's eyes flashed in anger. Even with Sue gone

142

she seemed to occupy all of Jeremy's thoughts. Jessica was getting sick of Jeremy's total disregard for her.

Jessica jumped up and stomped across the hot white pavement, determined to make him notice her. She was an expert swimmer, with an impeccable style and flawless technique. Jessica stopped as she reached the pool, making a show of climbing up the diving board and poising at the end of it. She dived high into the air, arcing her body gracefully and pointing her toes straight out behind her. Her graceful figure cut smoothly into the cool water, and she swam steadily across the length of the pool, bringing her arms above her head with strong, sure strokes.

Jessica climbed out of the pool and shook her hair, her tanned body smooth and glistening. She walked back to the chairs to find Jeremy snoring gently. Jessica bit her lip in frustration, feeling as if she were invisible. She shook her hair again, causing droplets of water to hit him. He blinked and opened his eyes.

"Oh, sorry," Jessica said, toweling herself off. "Did I wake you?"

"Oh, no, that's OK," said Jeremy, closing his eyes again.

"Jeremy, do you think you could put some lotion on my back?" Jessica asked, settling down on the chaise lounge and turning her back toward him.

"Sure, honey," said Jeremy agreeably. He pulled himself up and grabbed the suntan lotion from the deck. Jessica sat stiffly as he mechanically rubbed suntan lotion across her back. Well, she thought to herself, it looked as if she was going to have to pull out all the stops.

Jessica turned to face him. His body was so close to hers that she could feel the heat emanating from it. "Jeremy, I have something for you," she said softly, leaning under the chair and pulling out a small square box. She handed it to him silently.

"Wha—?" Jeremy said as he lifted the lid of the dark-blue velvet box. A thick gold band was nestled in the velvet. Jeremy sucked in his breath. "Jessica! You shouldn't have!" he exclaimed. "This must have cost a fortune."

"It was Steven's," Jessica explained. "He was once engaged to Cara Walker, but they broke it off. He thought we should have it." Steven hadn't actually given her permission to have the ring, but Jessica was sure he wouldn't notice its absence. And she was desperate to forge the bond that seemed to be rapidly disappearing between her and Jeremy.

"Here, try it on," said Jessica, her heart beating rapidly as she lifted the ring out of the setting. She tried to slip it onto his ring finger, but it didn't fit past his knuckle. Jessica could feel her face fall.

"Hey, it's OK," Jeremy said, looking at her tenderly. He put the ring on his pinkie finger, holding it up to display the perfect fit. The gold band sparkled in the sunlight. "This way it'll be even more special." Jessica was overcome with relief. She had been worried that he would reject her gesture.

Jessica's heart filled with love for Jeremy as she looked at him sitting next to her. His thick, tawny-blond hair was tangled and wavy from the

144

breeze, and his strong, dark body was glistening in the sun.

"Oh, Jeremy, I love you," Jessica said softly.

"I love you, too, Jessie," Jeremy said, pulling her into his arms and whispering in her ear. "More than anything in the world."

Chapter 12

"Where in the world are they?" said Todd to Lila as they waited for Robby and Sidney in the parking lot at Sweet Valley High during their lunch break.

Lila rolled her eyes. She felt as if she had heard that question a dozen times in the last five minutes. "Todd, do you mind? That question is beginning to get a little tiresome," Lila said in an insolent tone. She shifted uncomfortably, feeling constricted in her fitted suit and high heels under the hot sun. They were on their way to the SVP power plant to get uniforms, and they were outfitted for the occasion as young executives. Todd had on a business suit, and Lila was wearing an elegant scarlet suit with a matching hat. Lila lifted one foot out of a black pump and wriggled her toes around.

"Well, if they don't get here soon, we won't have time to get the equipment," Todd said worriedly. He pulled at his tie to loosen it. Lila gazed at Todd, taking in his attire with a critical eye. Todd was looking more conservative than ever in his navy-blue pin-striped suit. No wonder Jessica called him Mr. White Bread.

"Don't worry, they'll be here soon," Lila said in an aggravated tone. "Robby is extremely dependable." Lila pressed her fingers to her temples. Todd Wilkins and his constant moaning were beginning to get on her nerves.

"Sure he is," Todd muttered, kicking at some pebbles in the parking lot.

"Hey, there they are!" exclaimed Lila, waving at the approaching vehicle.

Robby pulled up to the sidewalk and rolled down the window. "Hi, good-looking, want a lift?" he asked Lila with a smile.

"Thanks, sailor," said Lila, jumping into the passenger seat and leaning over to give Robby a kiss.

"Hey, what about me?" asked Todd with a grin, his spirits lifting as he hopped into the backseat of the car.

"You're pretty good-looking too, Todd," said Robby with a smile. "But you're not my type. Sorry."

"Ah, well," said Todd with a grin. "Can't win 'em all."

"Lila, Todd, this is Sidney, my cousin. He's agreed to help us out," said Robby, introducing them to his cousin in the backseat.

"For a small fee, of course," joked Sidney from the back.

"Hi, Sidney," said Lila, twisting around to give him a welcoming smile. Sidney smiled back, his eyes crinkling as he did so. Lila looked from Robby to

Sidney. There was a definite family resemblance. They both had the same thick, black hair and piercing blue eyes. Of course, Sidney was wearing a beautiful charcoal-gray suit, and Robby was dressed as a starving artist in jeans and a T-shirt. Lila sighed, thinking how good Robby would look in a suit and tie.

"Nice to meet you, man," said Todd, holding out his hand to Sidney.

"You, too," said Sidney, shaking Todd's hand firmly.

"OK," said Robby, revving the motor and pulling out of the parking lot. "Now that the formalities are taken care of, it's time to get this show on the road." He pulled out onto the main road and put his foot on the accelerator.

Ten minutes later Robby pulled the car into the parking lot of a sprawling plant. The area was enclosed on all sides by a high metal fence, and a DANGER, HIGH VOLTAGE sign stood in front of the main gate.

"This is it, folks," said Robby, turning down the music.

"Sweet Valley Power," said Lila, reading the bold block letters highlighted across the building.

"Yep, SVP, the motor of Sweet Valley," said Sidney.

"OK," Todd said. "Now, is everybody set with the plan?" The other three nodded their heads solemnly.

"Good luck," said Robby as Todd, Lila, and Sidney jumped out of the car. "And remember, I'll be cruising the parking lot. If there's any trouble, just run for it and we'll make a quick getaway."

"Got it," said Todd, flashing a thumbs-up signal as he turned away from the car. Sidney accompanied Todd down the walk to the front door.

"Where's Lila?" Todd asked in exasperation as they reached the double doors. He stopped and looked back at the car. Lila was leaning down into the window, kissing Robby good-bye.

"Lila!" Todd called.

"Coming, coming!" Lila said, running across the gravel as best she could in her heels.

"Jeez, Lila, you're only going to be separated for about fifteen minutes," said Todd in an exasperated tone when she reached them.

"Oh, Todd, really," said Lila with a haughty shake of her hair, "sometimes you're so uptight."

"OK, guys, quiet down," cautioned Sidney as they entered the front door of the building. Two security guards sat behind a massive wooden desk.

"Right this way, please," said Sidney, adopting a formal tone as he ushered Todd and Lila to the desk. He took out his wallet and showed his SVP identification card to the guards.

"IDs, please," said the guard to Todd and Lila.

"These are special clients of mine," said Sidney with a self-assured smile. "We're going to do a tour of the plant." The guard nodded as Sidney signed them in as guests.

"Now, this is the main floor," said Sidney, indicating the area with a sweep of his arm. "The main floor houses the central switching station of the plant. To my right is the control room, the nerve center of the whole operation." He gestured to Lila and Robby to join him at the window overlooking a small room. "These men are monitoring different levels of energy output to make sure there isn't an energy overload or power surge."

"Very interesting," said Todd, playing along. "You know, our firm is particularly interested in examining the generator, where the power is produced."

"Certainly, certainly," boomed Sidney. "If you'll just accompany me to the elevators, we'll go to the engine room right now."

Sidney stepped up to the elevator bank and punched the button for the elevator. "Please, after you," said Sidney graciously, stepping back so they could get in first.

"Sidney, did you ever think of being a tour guide?" asked Lila as the elevator doors closed behind them.

"Or an actor?" added Todd.

Sidney gave them a beguiling smile. "I think corporate America is about all I'm good for."

The elevator stopped at the fourth floor and they stepped out. "Follow me," Sidney said, leading them down a long carpeted hall. A pair of SVP workers dressed in overalls passed them on their way.

Sidney stopped in front of a slatted wooden door and waited until the SVP workers had turned the corner. "OK," Sidney said in a low voice, drawing them toward him. "This is where the supplies are kept. Now, Lila, you're going to have to get the uniforms, because Todd and I will stand guard here and prevent anyone from entering."

"Sure, no problem," said Lila with false confidence. She ducked into the supply closet and shut the door behind her.

"Darnit!" Lila exclaimed, stumbling over a pile of linen in the small, dark room. She groped along the wall but couldn't find a light switch. She sat down on a mound of clothing and waited for a few moments. As soon as her eyes had adjusted to the dim light, she looked around the small room for a light.

"Aha!" said Lila to herself, noticing a string hanging from a light bulb in the ceiling. She pulled on the cord and blinked as the bright bulb illuminated the tiny room.

"Now, light-blue uniforms," said Lila, rummaging through the stacks of clothing piled up on shelves around the room. "Aprons, work shirts, towels—aha!" she said as she hit upon a stack of light-blue overall-type uniforms that the SVP electrical workers wore. She quickly sifted through the pile, checking the tags for sizes. She pulled out one small and two large and returned the stack to the corner.

Well, that wasn't so hard, thought Lila to herself, pleased with her work. She bent down to pick up the uniforms, but just as she was about to grab them, the door opened. Lila dived into the corner and burrowed deep underneath a pile of linen.

She peered through the cloth, trying to make out the form sharing the small space with her. It was an SVP worker looking for supplies. Lila held her breath as the worker rummaged around. She felt like a trapped animal, crouched underneath a pile of linen. Lila almost gasped out loud as the worker began walking straight toward her. *Ohmigod, what if he walks into me?* thought Lila in alarm. Lila's heart pounded as he stopped directly in front of her, reaching up onto a shelf on the wall to pick up a clean uniform. Finally he turned and walked to the door, giving the string a sharp tug before he left the room.

Lila exhaled heavily after he left, crawling quickly from her hiding place and waiting a few moments until the pounding in her chest subsided. She groped around in the dark on her knees until she felt the uniforms she had laid out.

Suddenly the door opened again and the light went on. Lila turned around quickly, feeling like a deer caught in a car's headlights. "Sidney!" she exclaimed, weak with relief.

"You OK?" he asked, reaching out a hand to help her up.

"Sure, no problem," said Lila, brushing off the knees of her panty hose as she stood up. She picked up the three uniforms and held them out to Sidney.

"C'mon, let's go," Sidney said, taking the extended pile of uniforms and shoving them into his empty leather briefcase.

Lila gave Todd a dirty look as she emerged, leading the way as the three of them walked quickly down the hall toward the elevator.

"I can't believe you let him in!" Lila burst out as soon as they were safely in the parking lot. She stared at Todd angrily, her eyes flashing with indignation.

"Sorry about that, Lila, but we couldn't stop him," Todd explained. "We told him the supply room was temporarily unavailable, but he said something about an emergency power failure and barged in."

"Yeah, Lila, we're really sorry," said Sidney apologetically. "We couldn't use force to stop him, because it would have looked too suspicious."

"But, Lila, you really saved the day," said Todd admiringly. "We thought for sure you'd get caught."

Lila smiled, feeling placated. She preferred this side of Todd to the whining drag he'd been all day.

"Yeah, Lila," put in Sidney. "How did you manage to hide in there?"

"Oh, I've got my ways," said Lila with a mysterious smile.

"The pool's great today!" exclaimed Jessica, munching loudly on a raw carrot. They were all gathered together in the den, picking at the sandwiches Elizabeth had prepared.

"Yeah, it's a beautiful day out," agreed Jeremy, taking a big bite out of his roast-beef sandwich.

Elizabeth looked at them in wonder. Why were they talking about the weather while her father was out obtaining ransom money for Sue's kidnapper? Jeremy was eating heartily, and Jessica was practically beaming.

"Liz, try to eat something," urged Mrs. Wakefield.

"Mom, I'm trying," said Elizabeth, taking a small bite of a turkey sandwich. The food seemed to stick in her throat. She put down the sandwich quickly and took a large gulp of water. "Hey, Dad's here!" she said as she heard the lock turn in the front door.

"Ned, how'd it go?" asked Mrs. Wakefield anxiously as Ned strode into the family room, a fat leather briefcase tucked underneath his arm.

"Everything went according to plan," said Mr. Wakefield, kneeling down and laying the briefcase carefully on the floor. "Now right here, in this little attaché case," he said, waving his hand with a flourish, "we've got the whole Gibbons family fortune, and then some." Everybody was silent as Mr. Wakefield rotated the dials on the lock. There was a small click, and the cover popped open an inch. While they all gathered around breathlessly, Mr. Wakefield slowly lifted the cover. Elizabeth looked at her father oddly, wondering why he was making such a production out of this.

Jessica gasped when her father opened the briefcase. It was crammed full with stacks of crisp green bills. "I've never seen so much money in my life," she breathed.

Elizabeth's eyes widened as well as she looked at the massive quantity of bills. After the secrecy of her parents' meeting with Sam this morning, she was surprised that her father was displaying the ransom money so openly.

"It's like in the movies!" Jessica exclaimed.

"Unfortunately, this is real life, Jess," said Elizabeth with a sigh.

Mr. Wakefield began pulling out stacks of bills and sorting through them, arranging them in piles of a hundred thousand dollars each.

"Let me help," said Jeremy, reaching out a hand for a pile of bills. Elizabeth watched as Jeremy counted through the money. He picked up a wad of bills and seemed to waft the print under his nose. *He's smelling the money*, Elizabeth realized. *He wants to make sure it's real.* For a fleeting moment Elizabeth thought she detected a self-satisfied smirk on Jeremy's face. But just as suddenly it was gone, and he looked completely serene and serious.

Mr. Wakefield counted out loud as soon as the money was sorted. "One hundred—two hundred—three hundred . . . six hundred thousand dollars," he said in satisfaction.

"Six hundred thousand dollars!" breathed Jessica. "That's over half a million dollars!"

"Nice work, Einstein," said Elizabeth wryly.

"Alice, I'm going to put this in the safety-deposit box until tonight," said Ned, packing up the briefcase and standing up. "And I'd like to confer with Sam as well. She's in the study, right?"

Mrs. Wakefield nodded. "I'll come with you," she said, jumping up and accompanying him to the study.

Elizabeth looked at Jeremy out of the corner of her eye after her parents had left the room. Why had he checked to see if the money was real? Was he hoping that it was fake, so that Sue wouldn't lose her fortune after all? Elizabeth watched him suspiciously as he picked up his sandwich and began eating energetically. He certainly wasn't acting as if he were worried about Sue *or* her inheritance.

As though he felt her looking at him, Jeremy put down his sandwich and returned her gaze. Elizabeth stared straight at him, an unspoken challenge in her bright-blue eyes.

Jeremy slowly averted his eyes. "So," he said, picking up Jessica's hand with total cool. "How about another dip?"

❋　　❋　　❋

"We're approaching the SVP garage," warned Sidney as he expertly steered Robby's car around a sharp turn. "Time to get in uniform, guys."

Todd looked nervously at the garage looming ahead of them. It was one thing to lift some uniforms, but quite another to steal a truck. He hoped Sidney knew what he was doing.

Lila picked up the uniforms off the dashboard. "Let the show commence," she said with a smirk, handing Todd and Robby their uniforms ceremoniously.

"Hey," Robby cautioned from the back. "No cheap thrills for you, young lady. I want you sitting straight ahead, your eyes concentrating on the smooth road in front of you."

"Yeah, Lila," Todd chimed in, "keep your wandering eyes to yourself."

"Believe me, Todd, that won't be a problem," said Lila wryly. "After all, I haven't eaten lunch yet today. I wouldn't want to lose my appetite."

Sidney burst out laughing from the driver's seat.

"Hey, hey!" Robby protested as he wriggled into the light-blue overalls. "Whose side are you on anyway, cous'?"

"You guys ready?" Sidney asked as they drove up the short driveway leading to the garage. "We've arrived. Lila, hit the deck." Lila crouched down in the front seat of the car and Sidney draped a coat over her. He coasted up to the gate and pulled smoothly to a stop.

Todd watched anxiously as Sidney flashed his card to the superintendent in the booth at the gate. This was the moment of truth. If they didn't get in now, the entire plan would be foiled.

"Going out for a site inspection?" asked the superintendent, checking out Robby and Todd in the back.

"Yeah, I'm sending the men out to the northwest sector. Seems to be some kind of water-main break," said Sidney.

"Bet the residents are gettin' antsy," said the superintendent in a gruff voice. He handed Sidney a key with a tag hanging from it and waved them through. "Truck eighty-four," he said.

Sidney maneuvered the car expertly through the sprawling indoor garage, steering around a series of winding ramps until they reached the eighth platform.

"Ain't she a beauty?" asked Sidney with a grin as they reached truck number eighty-four.

"Aren't you sweet?" said Lila, popping up at Sidney's words.

"She sure is," agreed Robby, looking with satisfaction at the shiny blue truck with the SVP logo on the side.

"Hrmmph," muttered Lila, looking out the window. Todd snorted derisively from the backseat, and Lila turned around and glared at him.

Robby took the keys from Sidney and hopped out of the car. Todd opened the door and tried to follow, but his right shoulder strap unbuckled as he stepped out, and his overalls dropped to his feet. Todd tripped and fell to the floor of the garage.

"Ohmigod!" said Lila, gasping with laughter. Todd

was sprawled on the ground in a pair of blue plaid boxer shorts, his overalls tangled around his ankles.

Lila unrolled the window and leaned out. "Todd, I'm really sorry," she said. "I guess I got the wrong size. But I like the boxers," she added with a smile.

"I'd like to box you," Todd muttered under his breath. He stood up quickly, his face flushing deeply as he hopped around pulling the overalls back up and fastening them securely. Todd sent Lila a withering look and climbed into the passenger side of the truck.

"We'll meet you guys back at Lila's," said Sidney, turning around to drive the car out. They had decided to stash the truck at the Fowler mansion, where it would be hidden from view.

"Yeah, see you soon," said Lila, ducking down in the front seat of the car. She popped up for a moment. "And, Todd, try to keep your pants on!" Lila added with a grin.

"Jessica, you're up first," Sam said.

Jessica stood up and rolled her eyes as the detective wrapped a thin bandage around her waist and taped a tiny transmitter to the small of her back. "I feel like I'm at the airport," Jessica complained, "except that I don't get the benefit of going anywhere."

"You could go to your room," offered Elizabeth.

"Very funny," said Jessica, wriggling around impatiently. "Just wait till you go through the inspection."

"Jessica, this isn't an inspection. Sam's bugging you," said Elizabeth in an exasperated tone.

"Sam's not bugging me," returned Jessica. "You are."

"Girls!" said Mrs. Wakefield sternly.

"Now, this will allow us to record everything at the drop-off. And I'll be able to hear you at all times," said Sam, running a wire from the transmitter around the front of Jessica's body. She then clipped a miniature mike to Jessica's shirt pocket. "Looks good," Sam said, patting Jessica on the arm. "Elizabeth, you're up next."

Jeremy gritted his teeth, watching with impatience while the detective attached a similar bug device to Elizabeth's clothing. He was anxious to find out the details for the evening's drop-off. They had all convened in the den after lunch to go over the plan, but Sam had insisted on taking every precaution before revealing her scheme.

"OK," Sam said, "you're all set. Now, remember, in case of an emergency, just speak into the microphone. I'll be able to pick up anything you say, and I'll be right behind you."

Finally, thought Jeremy to himself.

"OK, now here's the plan . . ." Sam said, speaking in a low voice. Jeremy leaned in closely to hear as she began to speak. "Jessica and Elizabeth will take the money in the Jeep and make the drop at the gas station. Then they'll pick up Sue. I'll follow behind at a safe distance."

"I don't know, Sam," interrupted Alice, shaking her head. "I'm not comfortable with the idea of using the kids as bait. The twins' lives could be endangered in this situation."

"Sam will be right behind them if there are any problems," said Mr. Wakefield in a reassuring tone.

"Alice, there's really nothing to worry about," said

Sam. "In cases like this the pickup people are rarely the targets of any violence."

Mrs. Wakefield nodded her head, trying to look convinced. "So then what?"

"Well, as soon as Sue is safely in the Jeep with the twins, I'll contact the authorities on my car phone and go after the kidnapper myself."

It's perfect, Jeremy thought to himself, his eyes glinting sharply. *Sam Diamond's plan will fit right into mine.*

Jeremy quickly revised Sam's plan in his head. The first order of business was to block up the tailpipe of Sam's car, so the engine would backfire. Jeremy would don his disguise and take her place following the twins as they went to make the drop. He would quickly overtake them and run them off the road—not enough to hurt them, but just enough to make them stop the car. While they were halted on the shoulder, Jeremy would jump in and grab the briefcase. And while the detective was checking out the wreck, Jeremy would make his getaway. And then he would be a rich man, thought Jeremy with glee. A very rich man.

But he would have to be extremely careful with this operation. Every second would count.

Chapter 13

"Liz, are you ready?" asked Jessica excitedly. It was six thirty on Tuesday night, a half hour before the drop-off time. Sam was waiting by the front door, holding her keys, and Mrs. Wakefield was pacing back and forth, wringing her hands together. Jeremy was slouched down in a chair in the foyer, his long legs crossed in front of him.

"I guess so," Elizabeth said, opening the front door and looking out at the dark night.

Jessica peeked out with her. It was pitch-black outside already, and the sky looked dark and ominous. "Liz, we're like Thelma and Louise, two renegades," Jessica whispered to her sister, her heart pounding with excitement. She felt as if she were on an important mission.

"Jess, we're not the outlaws. We're the victims," Elizabeth said, the anxiety evident in her voice.

"Oh, Liz," scoffed Jessica, "don't be such a worry-wart."

"Well, I'm glad you're enjoying this," said Elizabeth with a troubled sigh. "I'm terrified."

"C'mon, Liz," Jessica encouraged her, "try to get in the spirit of things. It's exciting. We're like Mata Hari out on a secret mission."

"Well, you certainly look the part," said Elizabeth wryly, indicating her attire. Jessica *had* dressed for the occasion, being careful to reattach the microphone to her new outfit. She was wearing tight black leggings with tiny purple stars on them and a matching deep-purple sweater. Her leggings were tucked into sleek black leather boots. A pair of cat-shaped black sunglasses completed the effect.

"I don't know what you're talking about," said Jessica innocently.

"You always wear sunglasses in the evening?" teased Elizabeth.

"I was just trying to be discreet!" said Jessica hotly. "We don't want to draw attention to ourselves at the scene of the crime."

"I don't know, Jess," said Jeremy, looking her over appreciatively. "You'll probably draw everybody's attention to yourself as soon as you pull into the gas station. In fact, I think you look too sexy to go out on the road. You might get stopped for distracting motorists."

"Oh, you're both ridiculous!" said Jessica, unable to resist a smile. She was glad that her efforts had paid off. At least Jeremy was beginning to notice her.

"Well, I wish I could stop you right here," said Jeremy, pulling Jessica down onto his lap. He wrapped a protective arm around her. "Promise you'll be careful?" he asked in a serious voice, lifting her chin up to look at him.

"Of course!" Jessica said, her eyes sparkling with excitement. "Nothing suits me better than danger and intrigue," she said, playing the part to the hilt. Actually, she thought, nothing suited her better than being the center of attention with an adoring man by her side.

"Well, I'm going to be thinking about you the whole time," said Jeremy, kissing her softly on the cheek.

Suddenly Mr. Wakefield appeared in the foyer, carrying the leather briefcase with him. "Liz, do you think you can handle this?" he asked, handing the briefcase to her.

Elizabeth swallowed hard. "Sure, Dad," she said, mustering a smile as she took the briefcase from him.

"I hope we don't get in an accident," said Jessica, looking at the briefcase in her sister's hands in awe. Elizabeth was carrying over half a million dollars in cash. And they were going to drive all the way across town with the money.

"That's the least of our worries," said Elizabeth.

Jeremy took Jessica by the hand and pulled her up off the steps. "Be safe, OK?" he whispered. "I'll be right here waiting for you when you get back." He kissed her tenderly and enfolded her in his arms.

"OK, girls, it's time to go," said Sam, looking at her watch. Sam picked up her jacket.

"My girls! My darling twin girls," Mrs. Wakefield cried, drawing Elizabeth and Jessica to her and hugging them both. Tears fell unabated down her cheeks.

"Mom, don't worry!" Jessica admonished. "We'll be fine!"

"I know, I know," said Mrs. Wakefield ruefully, laughing between her tears. She pulled her daughters closer to her.

"Mom, we've got to go," Jessica said, wriggling away.

"Be careful, girls," said Mr. Wakefield, kissing both his daughters on the cheek as they walked out the door.

Suddenly an object on the shelf in the foyer caught Jessica's eye. It was Amy Sutton's camcorder, the one she had used to make her film for the video club. Amy had left it at the Wakefields' by mistake. *Well, this might just come in handy,* thought Jessica, grabbing it impulsively as she left.

"Hey, Thelma, wait up!" she called, running after her sister to the Jeep.

"Wow, this truck is hard to maneuver," said Todd, peering over the steering wheel of the SVP truck at the road below. He didn't know why he'd offered to drive. The way he was handling the van, they'd be lucky if they made it to the Wakefields' house alive. The truck lurched wildly as he swung it around the corner onto Calico Drive.

"Jeez, I feel like a kid on a roller-coaster ride!" moaned Lila from the passenger seat, holding her stomach with her hand.

"Well, you *look* like a man in uniform," said Robby

with a grin, reaching over the seat to lay a hand on her shoulder. Lila had fastened a fake mustache to her upper lip and had pulled her hair back in a white painter's cap. They were all wearing SVP uniforms and had smudged their faces with dirt to conceal their identities.

"Hey, Todd, why don't you slow down here so we can get ready?" suggested Lila.

"But gently, man, gently," cautioned Robby.

Todd shifted gears carefully and pressed the brake slowly, but the van stalled and lurched to a sudden stop. "Oh, well, we've stopped at least," sighed Todd. He unbuckled his seat belt and turned to face Lila and Robby. "Robby, can you hand us the gear from the back of the truck?"

Robby twisted around and pulled out a pile of equipment. "Fire extinguisher for the lady," he said, handing the small red apparatus to Lila.

Lila took the flame retardant and turned it around, carefully studying the device. She turned on the car light and quickly read the instructions on the label. "Looks easy enough," she said, flicking off the light.

"A tool belt, cable wire, and a flashlight," Robby said, handing the goods to Todd. Todd fastened the tool belt around his waist and fit the wire and flashlight into two empty slots.

"And an industrial tool kit for me," Robby said, placing a steel-gray tool kit by his side.

"OK, guys, this is it," said Todd, his heart beginning to beat as he looked at the house down the street. He turned the engine, and the truck pitched forward to a start.

                    ❈   ❈   ❈

Jeremy stood with the Wakefields at the front door,
watching as the girls pulled away in the Jeep. He fought
the urge to run after them immediately and jump into
his own car. But he didn't want to draw attention to
himself. Instead he took a deep breath and forced himself to count to ten before he sprang into action.

"I'm worried about them," Jeremy said in a low
voice.

"We are too, Jeremy," said Mrs. Wakefield solemnly.

"You know what? I'm not of any use here,"
Jeremy said suddenly. He slapped his hand to his
forehead as if struck by an idea. "I know! I'll wait in
the Nature Cabin. That way I'll be closer to the action if there are any problems."

"That's an idea," said Mr. Wakefield. "In fact, why
don't I come—"

But Jeremy was already out the door. "Call me
there if you need me!" Jeremy cried, sprinting across
the lawn before Ned Wakefield could join him. He
yanked a wool ski mask out of his pocket and pulled it
over his face as he ran.

"There's someone at the door!" Todd cried, noticing a shadowy figure dart out of the front door of the
Wakefield house and disappear into the darkness. He
pulled the truck up to the sidewalk and abruptly cut
the engine. The truck hurled forward and rattled to a
stop.

"It's the kidnapper!" exclaimed Lila.

"C'mon, you guys, forget the plan, let's get him!"
said Todd.

"You're on, man," said Robby, scrambling out of the truck. Lila and Todd jumped out after him and ran full speed onto the lawn. Todd and Robby came in from opposite sides and jumped onto the kidnapper.

"Aarggh!" yelled the masked figure, flinging his arms around wildly. He deftly wriggled out of their hold and darted to the left.

"Double-team him!" called Todd. Robby jumped on him from behind and Todd grabbed his flailing arms. He pulled out the cable wire from his tool belt and tried to wrap it around the kidnapper's arms. "Lila!" Todd squeaked out as the kidnapper struggled wildly.

Holding the fire extinguisher upright, Lila pulled the pin and pressed the lever, directing the spray with full force at the kidnapper's face and body.

The kidnapper reeled from the force of the spray and stumbled to the ground. Robby and Todd jumped on him. Todd held his legs while Robby climbed on top of him and pinned him firmly to the ground in a wrestler's hold.

"We got him!" Todd exclaimed.

Robby leaned over and pulled the ski mask off the kidnapper's face. "Jeremy!" he breathed in amazement.

"Would you get off me?" Jeremy sputtered, his face purple with rage. Todd let go of his hold, and Robby jumped up and stumbled back across the lawn. Jeremy stood up and shook out his hair furiously. His clothes were drenched and his long blond hair was wild, matted and tangled from the flame retardant.

"Ohmigod, Jeremy, I'm so sorry," said Lila, pulling

off her cap and letting her hair fall around her shoulders. "We didn't mean to get you."

"Uh, yeah, sorry about that," chimed in Todd, staring at Jeremy in dismay. Jeremy looked like a drowned rat, with droplets of water running from his tousled hair onto his face. Todd hung his head in despair. They had gone after the wrong man. Now they would never be able to free the Wakefields.

"Just get out of my way, would you?" Jeremy snapped, shoving Todd out of the way and running to his car.

Todd looked after him, bewildered. "It was just an accident," he said.

"Well, I guess he didn't like the greeting," said Robby wryly.

"Why was he wearing that ski mask?" wondered Lila.

"Maybe it's some kind of Halloween costume," surmised Robby. "Maybe he wanted to scare Jessica or something."

"What's going on here?" demanded Mr. Wakefield, running out of the house with Mrs. Wakefield fast in tow. "What's all the commotion?" Todd stared at them as they emerged from the house, stunned to see the Wakefields waltzing out onto their lawn free and unharmed. Where was the kidnapper? And why had Jeremy run away in such a hurry?

"Uh, hi, Mr. and Mrs. Wakefield," said Lila with a small wave of her hand.

"Lila, is that you?" said Mr. Wakefield, peering at her face.

"Yeah, it's me," said Lila with a sigh.

"Lila? Todd?" said Mrs. Wakefield. She looked at Robby in confusion. "And you're an SVP worker?"

"No, Mrs. Wakefield, this is Robby," Lila said, looking down at the ground. "Robby is my, uh, boyfriend."

"I see," said Mrs. Wakefield. "Well, hi, Robby." She looked back and forth from the SVP truck to the kids in uniforms. "What in the world are you doing with this equipment? And these outfits?"

"We, uh, we thought you were being held hostage," stuttered Todd. Todd flashed Lila an angry look. He felt like slaughtering her. He had been so worried, and the Wakefields had been fine all along. He should have known that this was all just some stupid story that Jessica had concocted.

"You thought we were being held hostage?" repeated Mrs. Wakefield.

"Now, where did you get that idea?" asked Mr. Wakefield.

"Well, uh, Jes—" Todd started to explain, but he stopped quickly, realizing he could get the twins into trouble. Not that he would mind if Jessica was punished for the unnecessary worry she had caused him, but he didn't know if Elizabeth was involved as well. Until he found out what all of this was about, he was going to keep his mouth shut.

Todd looked at Lila gratefully as she took over. "We got worried when Jessica and Elizabeth weren't in school and wouldn't take our calls," Lila explained smoothly, "so we came by here to see if they were in danger. And we thought we saw a strange man inside, so . . ." Lila's voice trailed off.

"So we jumped to the conclusion that your family

171

was being held hostage," finished Todd lamely.

"I see," said Mrs. Wakefield, a skeptical look on her face. "Well, I don't know about the story," she said, shaking her head, "but your intentions were good. Why don't you come in to get cleaned up?"

"Thanks, Mrs. Wakefield," Todd said, giving her an appreciative smile.

"But what about the truck? The uniforms? What were you trying to accomplish?" asked Mr. Wakefield.

"Well, it's kind of a long story," began Todd.

"Why don't you explain inside?" suggested Mrs. Wakefield, putting her arms around Lila and Todd and leading them to the house. "But, Lila," she said, turning to face her with a smile, "don't you think you should take off that mustache first?"

Chapter 14

"Get out of my way," Jeremy growled, honking loudly at a blue Datsun approaching the intersection. He careened through the red light, causing the small blue car to slam on its breaks and swerve off the road.

"Idiot," Jeremy muttered at the blue car halted by the roadside. He slammed his foot onto the accelerator and turned off the highway sharply, hugging the curve tightly as he exited Route 44. He turned onto a side road and cut his speed.

Jeremy coasted up behind the minimart at the Glen's Grove gas station and slowed to a stop. He inched around the building slowly until the lot came into view. The twins' black Jeep was sitting in the gas station by the telephone booth. "Darnit!" Jeremy exclaimed, slamming his fist against the dashboard. He was too late. Jessica and Elizabeth were already there, waiting for Sue to appear. Now there was no way he could get the money and make a clean getaway.

Jeremy rubbed his fingers against his throbbing temples. *It's just a setback,* he told himself, trying to get his thoughts together. He closed his eyes and concentrated deeply.

That's it! he said out loud, suddenly hit with the perfect plan. It looked as if he was going to have to get Sue involved. Things were going to be more complicated than he would have liked, but it could still work. And he could still be a rich man in a matter of days. Jeremy revved the engine and backed up rapidly around the building, his wheels screeching as he turned onto the road.

Sue's eyes lit up as she heard Jeremy's car pull into the gravel driveway. She had been tied to the hard wooden chair all day and was aching for some relief. Jeremy hadn't stopped by at all since the morning. She was weak with hunger, and the pain in her muscles and joints was becoming unbearable.

"Sue!" Jeremy bellowed as he marched into the cabin and slammed the door behind him, causing a picture to fall off the wall.

The sound of Jeremy's furious voice sent a tremor down Sue's body. She quickly stuffed the bandanna into her mouth and tried to return his call. "Mmpphh!" Sue called from the attic.

Sue could hear Jeremy yank open the trapdoor and pull down the wooden staircase. The sound of his footsteps pounding up the creaky attic steps filled her with fear. Sue huddled in her chair as Jeremy marched into the room and turned on the light.

Something must have gone terribly wrong to have sent him into such a rage.

"C'mon, we're late," Jeremy said, pulling the bandanna out of her mouth and shoving it into his pocket. He deftly untied the ropes binding her and threw them in a pile on the floor.

"Jeremy, what happened?" Sue exclaimed, leaning over to massage her legs where the rope had cut into them. She stretched her arms above her head and rubbed her wrists and ankles briskly.

"I'll explain later," Jeremy said gruffly. "Now, c'mon!" He yanked her out of the chair, and Sue collapsed onto the floor, her cramped muscles weak from lack of movement.

"Sorry!" Sue exclaimed. She huddled on the floor and looked up at Jeremy with frightened eyes.

"That's OK," Jeremy said, taking a deep, ragged breath. He knelt down and helped her up, walking a few steps with her as her muscles adjusted to the movement. "Now, do you think you can make it?" he asked.

Sue nodded silently and followed him cautiously down the attic steps. As they walked to the back door of the cabin, she hesitated. She remembered her resolve to get herself out of this horrible situation. She had to call a stop to the plan now, before it was too late. She couldn't let Jeremy scare her into submission again.

"Jeremy!" Sue said, stopping suddenly before they reached the door.

Jeremy turned around and stared at her. "What is it now?" he growled, looking at her in annoyance.

Sue took a deep breath. "I—I don't think we should go through with this. Nobody knows we're involved, and nobody will catch on. I'll say I was lost, or kidnapped, or whatever—and then we'll go back to New York and get on with our lives."

"Sue, I told you, it's too late now," Jeremy said, a muscle twitching in his cheek.

Sue stared at him stubbornly. "Jeremy, you can do whatever you like. You can get the money any way you want, but I refuse to be involved with it!" she declared, her hands on her hips.

Jeremy stared at her in disbelief. "Sue, I can't do this without you," he said. "You know that."

"Well, then, you'll have to come up with a new plan," Sue said, "because I'm not going!" She sat down hard in the chair and looked up at him defiantly.

"Would you like me to force you into the car?" Jeremy asked in a quiet, controlled voice. His tone was menacing and his eyes were glazed. Sue looked up at him quickly. Something in his eyes made her shake her head no. She wasn't quite sure what he would do if she disobeyed him.

"No, it's just—I—" Sue stammered, her voice timid.

"Get in the car!" Jeremy yelled, his voice breaking. He grabbed a felt hat from the coatrack and yanked her up. Sue stumbled along, shaking and crying, as he pulled her to the car. He opened the passenger door and shoved her in.

Jeremy sped along the familiar route, hugging the dirt roads. He turned into a back road and pulled up again behind the minimart at the gas station. Sue

176

was huddled against the window in the car.

"Would you stop your bawling?" Jeremy asked in disgust.

"S-sorry," Sue said, her voice trembling.

"Well, this is it, lady," Jeremy said harshly, leaning over and opening the passenger door. "Rescue time."

Sue nodded and stared straight ahead, tears falling in streams down her cheeks. She was about to commit a terrible crime, which she would carry around for the rest of her life, and she was going to betray the people who had been kindest to her. All she would have left was Jeremy, who had turned into a total stranger.

"Sue, you've got to get out of the car!" Jeremy exploded, practically pushing her out the door. Sue stumbled out of the car and hobbled across the gravel.

Jeremy jumped out of the car and went to her. He knelt in front of her and took her hands in his. "Sue, Sue, honey, please, I'm sorry if I've been mean. It's just so hard having you turn on me like this."

"Oh, Jeremy, I'm sorry, too," said Sue, falling into his arms. "I didn't mean to betray you."

"That's OK, sweetheart," Jeremy said, wiping her tears from her cheeks. "Feel better now?"

Sue nodded and sniffled.

"Now, get yourself together, honey," said Jeremy softly. "I'll pick you up tonight at eight from the Wakefields', and then we'll make our getaway. You'll need to wait outside. Do you think you can do that?"

"Yes, I think so," Sue said quietly.

"And remember, by this time tomorrow we'll be

safe and sound in Mexico," Jeremy said, chucking her chin. "Sound good?"

Sue nodded and mustered a weak smile.

"Jess! There she is!" exclaimed Elizabeth. She trembled with joy at the sight of her friend, waves of relief coursing through her body. Sue was standing by a gas pump at the far end of the gas station. She looked like a wreck, her hair tangled and her clothes—she was still in her witch costume—ragged, but she seemed unharmed. *For the moment at least,* Elizabeth thought grimly.

"She looks like she's been through a war," Jessica breathed.

"She has," said Elizabeth. Her heart went out to Sue. She looked totally defenseless, a small, forlorn figure standing alone in the still night.

"Well, this is it," said Elizabeth, closing her hand firmly around the briefcase handle.

"Good luck, Liz," whispered Jessica, readying the camera.

"Thanks, Jess," said Elizabeth, opening the door with trembling fingers and sliding out of the Jeep. She held the briefcase firmly in her hand and made her way quickly across the gravel. Elizabeth spoke quietly into the microphone as she walked. "Sam, I'm on my way to do the drop," she said. "Sue's here, but there's no sign of the kidnapper yet." Elizabeth felt completely vulnerable in the open air, expecting to be grabbed or shot at any moment.

Time seemed to stop as Elizabeth crossed the few yards separating her from the telephone booth. The whole scene was completely surreal. Sue was standing perfectly still across the lot, and Elizabeth was carrying over half a million dollars in her hands.

Finally Elizabeth reached the telephone booth. Tremors racked her body as she pushed open the glass door. She set the briefcase carefully inside and backed out quickly. At that moment a man darted in from nowhere and grabbed the briefcase. Elizabeth jumped back and hightailed it to the car, the pounding of her heart filling her ears.

She ducked into the passenger seat and slammed the door shut. Leaning her head back against the seat, she drew a deep breath, relieved to be back in the security of the Jeep. Now they just had to pick up Sue. And then Sam would go after the kidnapper.

Elizabeth looked around the gas station, wondering where Sam was. "Jess, where's Sam?" she asked. "She should have been here by now. The guy's going to get away."

"Mmm, I don't know," Jessica mumbled. She was crouched down in her seat, steadily taping the entire scene.

"Sam, where are you?" said Elizabeth in an urgent tone, turning her mouth toward the microphone. "He's still in the booth." Elizabeth watched with a mixture of horror and fascination as the kidnapper paused in the phone booth. He appeared to be studying the contents of the briefcase. He was about six feet tall and was wearing a long trench coat, a gray felt hat, and dark sunglasses. Elizabeth tried to make out his features, but a red bandanna covered his face. The man clicked the briefcase shut and left the phone booth. Once in the open air, he ran across the lot and disappeared behind the building.

Elizabeth watched carefully as Sue began hobbling across the lot after the kidnapper was out of sight. But before she had gone a few feet, her knees buckled underneath her, and she collapsed in a heap by the gas pump.

"Jess, she's hurt!" cried Elizabeth, leaping out of the Jeep and running to her. Jessica jumped out and followed her.

"Sue, are you OK? What hurts?" Elizabeth asked in alarm as she reached her. She knelt down by the girl.

Sue remained crouched on the ground, trembling in silence.

"Sue, have you been shot? Have you been wounded?" pressed Elizabeth. "Please, tell me where it hurts." Elizabeth began to cry. She didn't know if she should stay with Sue or call an ambulance.

"No, no, I'm fine," Sue managed finally. "I'm not hurt. I'm just weak and stiff. From the ropes . . ."

Elizabeth went weak with relief as the tension eased out of her body. "Ssh, don't think about it," she said, putting her arms around the girl and hugging her. "You're all right now. You're safe and sound and with people who love you."

Sue gave Elizabeth a short hug in return and quickly disentangled herself from the embrace. It was clear that she had been through an ordeal, thought Elizabeth as she took in Sue's pale, wan face. Her cheeks were streaked with grime, and her eyes were red and puffy.

Just at that moment Sam sped into the gas station in Mr. Wakefield's rust-brown LTD. She skidded to a stop by them and jumped out of the car.

"Sam!" Elizabeth exclaimed. "What happened to you? The kidnapper got away!"

"Why did you take Dad's car?" Jessica asked.

"Someone stuffed a rag in the tailpipe of my car, so the engine wouldn't start. I had to take your father's car," Sam explained, her expression grim. "But I lost precious time figuring out what the problem was." She shook her head ruefully. "Whoever he is, he's smart."

Suddenly Elizabeth noticed Sue's baffled expression. "Sue, this is Sam," Elizabeth said. "She's a private detective, and she's been working on your case."

"Nice to meet you," said Sue in a tiny voice.

"Well, what happened?" Sam asked. "Did you manage to do the drop?"

Jessica and Elizabeth quickly filled her in on the details of the drop-off. "So basically everything went according to plan," concluded Elizabeth.

"Except for the fact that the kidnapper got off scot-free," said Jessica.

"Well, at least you're all safe and sound," said Sam as she put her arm around Sue and led her to the car. "All's not lost."

"No, just six hundred thousand bucks," Jessica said.

"Oh, I don't think that's really a problem," said Sam with a smile.

Jessica's mouth dropped open. "Not a problem?" she exclaimed.

"But that was Sue's entire inheritance!" Elizabeth chimed in.

"The money was fake," Sam explained. "Your father got counterfeit bills from the bank for the occasion. Under my authorization." Jessica's eyes popped open, and Elizabeth noticed Sue smile for the first time since the rescue.

Chapter 15

"Lila! Robby!" Jessica exclaimed as she and Elizabeth walked into the living room.

"Todd!" Elizabeth squealed at the same time. "What are you doing here?"

Todd didn't say anything. He just pulled her into his arms and engulfed her in a huge bear hug. Todd looked at her tenderly when they pulled back. "Oh, Liz, I was so worried about you," he said, his eyes moist.

"You knew?" Elizabeth asked in surprise. "But how? Who told you?"

Todd flicked his head in the direction of Jessica, who was talking animatedly with Lila and Robby in the corner.

"That figures," Elizabeth said, her hands on her hips. "It's impossible to keep anything a secret around here."

"Well, it doesn't matter now," said Todd, drawing her into his arms. "All that matters is that you're home and safe."

Elizabeth leaned into Todd's arms contentedly. "Oh, Todd, I missed you so much," she said. "It was awful going through this without you."

Suddenly she pulled back as she became aware of Todd's light-blue SVP overalls. "Todd, what are you wearing?" she asked.

Todd grinned. "Oh, just a standard SVP worker uniform," he said, indicating Lila's and Robby's matching attires.

"What the—?" began Elizabeth.

"Jessica! Elizabeth!" cried Mr. and Mrs. Wakefield in unison, walking into the room at that moment. Mrs. Wakefield had insisted on following Sam in her car, but the gas station had been deserted when they arrived.

Mrs. Wakefield opened her arms to the girls, hugging them both to her. "You're OK."

Suddenly she looked around the room, a panicked look in her eyes. "Where's Sue?" she asked.

"She's fine, Mom," Elizabeth said quickly. "She's driving back with Sam."

Just then the back door opened and Sam walked in, a bedraggled Sue by her side. "Oh, Sue!" said Mrs. Wakefield, hugging the girl to her. "We've been so worried about you." Tears of joy streamed down Mrs. Wakefield's face.

"Now, don't go getting kidnapped again," said Mr. Wakefield with mock sternness, giving Sue a quick hug as well.

"I'll do my best not to, Mr. Wakefield," said Sue, smiling.

❀   ❀   ❀

Jessica looked around the room, wondering where Jeremy was. He had said he would be there waiting when they got back. Jessica had walked in the door beaming, expecting a hero's welcome. Instead she had found boring Todd Wilkins and Lila's lovey-dovey boyfriend Robby. Why wasn't Jeremy there? wondered Jessica. Wasn't he worried about her?

Jessica took in the joyful scene, aggravated by the merriment around her. The happy family reunion was beginning to irritate her. Everybody was laughing happily and hugging each other, thrilled to have annoying Sue back. *Great,* Jessica thought, falling into an armchair dejectedly. *Sue's back and Jeremy's gone.*

Jessica could hear her mother cooing by her side. She looked at the tender scene between Mrs. Wakefield and Sue in annoyance. Mrs. Wakefield was sitting by Sue's side, gently patting her hair. Jessica tugged on her mother's arm. "Where's Jeremy?" she asked when her mother looked up.

"Oh, he's at the cabin," Mrs. Wakefield explained. "He wanted to be closer to the action." She ruffled her daughter's hair. "Don't worry, dear. I'm sure he'll be back soon."

Jessica ducked away from her mother's hand and ran up the steps to her room. She fell onto the bed on her stomach and picked up the phone, quickly punching in the number of the cabin. Nestling the phone in the crook of her neck, she rested her head in her hands and stared at the wall dejectedly as the phone rang.

"No answer, of course," she muttered to herself, slamming down the receiver.

185

⁂

"Everybody in the kitchen!" ordered Mrs. Wakefield. "Cocoa and cake for the returning heroes."

Elizabeth led the way as everybody piled into the kitchen. They all took seats around the table while Mr. and Mrs. Wakefield prepared snacks. Elizabeth jumped up to help her parents, bringing a stack of paper plates and napkins to the table.

"Well, it's a regular shindig, isn't it?" Jessica said as she walked into the kitchen a moment later. She jumped up onto a kitchen stool and grabbed a cup of hot chocolate from the tray set on the counter.

It is *like a party,* thought Elizabeth to herself, looking at her family and friends crowded around the kitchen table. Everybody was talking at once. It seemed as if they all had a different story to tell and were all telling it at the same time.

"Well, I think you're all heroes," Mrs. Wakefield declared, bringing steaming cups of hot chocolate to the table on a tray. She set out a strawberry shortcake and a carton of vanilla ice cream on the butcher-block table.

Mr. Wakefield followed with a bottle of Chablis. He poured two glasses of wine for himself and Alice. "We deserve it," he said to the group with a sheepish grin. "We've been through a lot."

"Who wants a big piece?" asked Mrs. Wakefield as she began slicing the cake and passing around pieces. Todd and Robby raised their hands.

"Now, I know you've probably been through this already," said Mr. Wakefield, adding scoops of ice cream to the plates, "but I haven't heard the details of the drop-off yet."

As they ate, Jessica and Elizabeth updated everybody on the events of the drop-off, from the moment they pulled into the gas station to Sam's arrival in Mr. Wakefield's car. "So it all worked out in the end," concluded Elizabeth. "Sue's safe and sound and so is her money."

"And now we've just got to identify the kidnapper," added Jessica. "And fortunately, we've got it all on tape—"

Sue choked on her cake and dropped her fork. The utensil fell off the table and clattered loudly on the floor. "Excuse me," she said, her face turning red as she retrieved her silverware.

"You're just jumpy from the whole ordeal," said Elizabeth, turning to Sue with a smile. "But as soon as we find the kidnapper, the nightmare will really be over."

"Uh-huh," Sue said. She didn't even look up from her food. She was concentrating fully on her plate, steadily eating her cake and ice cream. It looked to Elizabeth as if she hadn't eaten in days.

"Hey, Sue, did the kidnapper starve you, or what?" asked Jessica. Elizabeth sent her a sharp look. Sometimes Jessica could be so insensitive.

"Almost," Sue said, swallowing the last bit of cake and licking the remaining crumbs from the fork. "He gave me some bread in the morning and some water during the day."

Mrs. Wakefield gasped. "But that's torture!" she exclaimed, slicing another piece of cake and putting it on her plate.

"Mom, you're like Marie Antoinette." Elizabeth

laughed. "Maybe we should give Sue some real food."

"No, I'm fine," said Sue, holding up a hand. "I'll just have some fruit," she said, picking out a banana from the fruit bowl in the middle of the table. "What I'm really looking forward to is a good night's sleep."

"Sue had to sleep tied up in a wooden chair in the cabin," explained Mrs. Wakefield, recounting the information that Sue had given them earlier.

"I know what that's like," said Elizabeth sympathetically, remembering her experience as a prisoner in Carl's cabin when she had been kidnapped. She had slept upright in a chair for two nights while her captor had snored comfortably in his bed in the other room.

"So you didn't see the kidnapper at all, Sue?" asked Mr. Wakefield.

"No, I didn't even catch a glimpse of him," Sue said, shaking her head regretfully. "He grabbed me from behind while I was taking a walk outside and covered my eyes with some sort of cloth. I was blindfolded the whole time."

"Well, we've got him on tape now," said Mr. Wakefield reassuringly. "We'll find him in no time."

"I propose a toast," declared Mrs. Wakefield, raising her wine flute in the air. "To Elizabeth—for successfully completing the drop-off," she began, raising her glass in Elizabeth's direction. "To Jessica—for fearlessly taping the entire event; to Lila, Todd, and Robby—for their courageous rescue attempt; and most of all, to Sue," she finished solemnly, "for her bravery in the face of this ordeal."

"Hail, hail the conquering heroes!" chimed in Mr.

Wakefield, waving his glass wildly in the air. They all laughed and clinked glasses.

"Well, there's one thing I still don't understand," said Elizabeth. "Why is there an SVP truck in our driveway, and why are you all dressed like SVP workers?"

Elizabeth's question sent everybody into gales of laughter again. When the laughter finally died down, Mrs. Wakefield wiped away her tears and explained what their friends had been up to. Todd and Lila had told Mr. and Mrs. Wakefield the whole story.

Elizabeth looked at Sue curiously while her mother talked. She was the only one who didn't seem happy. In fact, she seemed close to despair. She was gazing toward the front door, a despondent look on her face. *Well, maybe she's still in shock,* thought Elizabeth to herself.

"So then Todd and Lila came over and spied on the house. And after they saw the kidnapper, they were sure we were all being held hostage," continued Mrs. Wakefield, laughing at the outlandish possibility.

"That must have been Jeremy," put in Jessica, squirming uncomfortably.

She must be scared that she's in trouble for telling Lila about the kidnapping, thought Elizabeth to herself. Elizabeth watched as Jessica looked at Lila nervously, lifting an inquiring eyebrow.

"Don't worry," Lila mouthed, sending Jessica a reassuring look.

Elizabeth smiled to herself. She had been so worried about revealing anything to Todd, and he had known what was going on all along. Oh, well, she thought to herself in amusement, at least one thing would always be constant—Jessica would always be Jessica.

"OK, folks, this is our last order of business," said Sam, popping the videocassette into the VCR. "Identifying the kidnapper." She had waited until the twins' friends left after dessert before showing the video.

Elizabeth settled back against the couch, looking around the room contentedly. Jessica was lying on the rug on her stomach, her parents were sitting together cozily on the love seat, and Sue was curled up in an armchair. It didn't even matter if they couldn't identify the kidnapper, thought Elizabeth to herself. All that counted was that Sue was back and her family was safe.

Jessica let out a whistle as Elizabeth appeared on the screen. "Wow, Liz, you're pretty photogenic," she said. The shot showed Elizabeth walking across the lot with the briefcase, her steps strong and her head held high.

"She owes it all to you, Jessica," said Mrs. Wakefield. "You're the director of this movie."

"Yeah, Jess, you should be a filmmaker," said Elizabeth, impressed with the quality of the tape. Jessica had captured every detail of the drop-off: Elizabeth placing the briefcase in the telephone booth, the kidnapper darting into the screen, Elizabeth jumping out of his way, the kidnapper examining the contents of the briefcase, and a shot of the retreating figure from the back.

"He sure is greedy," said Mr. Wakefield after the tape had played through. "He risked precious time confirming the authenticity of the money."

"He may be greedy, but he's not very professional," put in Sam. "Not if that money fooled him."

"Well, does anybody recognize him?" asked Mrs. Wakefield.

"He kind of looks like John Pfeifer," offered Jessica.

"Jessica!" Elizabeth protested. "Where's the resemblance?"

"Well, he's about six feet tall, well built, a man . . ." Jessica said.

"That's totally outrageous," Elizabeth scoffed. "You're just saying that because you don't like him."

"Well, he did try to date-rape my best friend," said Jessica defensively.

"That doesn't mean he kidnapped Sue!" said Elizabeth.

"OK, OK," Jessica said. "Any other suggestions?" Everybody shook their heads.

"You know, Jessica's pointing to the real problem with this man's identity," put in Sam. "He's very typical looking. Mug shots wouldn't help. A hundred convicted men would fit his description."

"Well, let's watch it through again," Mr. Wakefield said, rewinding the tape. "We'll run it through in slomo this time."

They watched again as Elizabeth made her way painstakingly across the lot in slow motion. Elizabeth studied the screen closely. But all she saw was herself. Every gesture was slow and leaden,

191

creating the impression that she was swimming across the lot.

"I can't find any clue to his identity whatsoever!" exclaimed Elizabeth in frustration after the tape had played through again.

"Why don't we freeze-frame some of the shots this time?" suggested Sam, picking up the clicker from the table. She rewound the tape and began playing it through, stopping it every time the kidnapper appeared in the frame at a different angle.

As Sam ran through the shots of the kidnapper, Elizabeth realized that Sue had been strangely quiet the whole time the tape had been playing. Of all the people in the room, Sue would have been the most likely to have some information to offer about the identity of the kidnapper. But, then, thought Elizabeth, she had been gagged and blindfolded the whole time. Maybe replaying the drop-off was causing her to relive the entire experience.

Elizabeth looked over at Sue, worried that the video was causing her pain. But Sue wasn't even looking at the TV screen. In fact, she seemed strangely preoccupied. She kept looking at her watch and glancing toward the front door.

"Sue, is something the matter?" Elizabeth asked her gently.

"What?" Sue asked, jumping at Elizabeth's voice. "Oh, no, no," she said as Elizabeth's question registered. "I guess I'm just nervous from the whole ordeal. In fact, I think I need to get some air."

Sue jumped up abruptly. "I'll be back in a sec!" she said, picking up her coat and bag and running out the front door. Elizabeth watched her retreating figure with a bewildered expression on her face.

Sue paced back and forth in front of the Wakefield house, relieved to have made it outside. She hadn't seen anything incriminating on the tape, but it had made her nervous watching it. At least it would all be over soon, Sue thought to herself. Jeremy would be arriving any minute for their getaway. Within an hour they would be on a plane to Mexico and then to Rio, far away from the Wakefields and the kidnapping and crime. Sue couldn't wait to leave Sweet Valley for good. She wasn't particularly thrilled about accompanying Jeremy, but she didn't have much choice at this point. She really was in too deep to back out now.

Sue shivered and pulled her coat tightly around her as a breeze drifted through the air and ruffled her hair. She looked down at her watch. Eight fifteen. Jeremy was fifteen minutes late. *Where is he?* she thought in consternation. If she stayed out there any longer, the Wakefields would get suspicious. Or worried. In any case, they were sure to come out looking for her. Sue ran to the end of the block and looked down the deserted street. There was no sign of him. She walked dejectedly back to the house and plopped down on the curb.

Sue put her head in her hands and thought dreamily about the future. The discovery that the money was fake had come as a tremendous relief to her. The future looked bright again. Now she didn't have to carry around the burden of guilt for the rest of her life.

Maybe things would get better with Jeremy, thought Sue optimistically. He would be furious when he found out the money was fake, but he would get over it. It was only driving them apart, anyway. When they got back to New York, everything would be good again. They would be together as they always had been, without all this plotting and scheming. This whole ordeal with the Wakefields would finally be behind them, and they would be able to get on with their lives.

Sue looked at her watch again. Eight thirty. *That's odd*, she thought. *Jeremy is never late.* And especially not when half a million dollars was involved. He'd executed every aspect of the entire plan with minute precision. Suddenly Sue was hit with a realization, a horrible realization. Jeremy wasn't coming back for her. And he'd never been planning to. He had fooled Jessica all along. And he had fooled her as well.

"Sue, where have you been?" Elizabeth exclaimed as Sue walked back into the family room.

"Oh, I was just sitting outside, enjoying the calm of the evening," said Sue, sitting down again in the armchair. Elizabeth looked at her closely. Sue had a strangely serene expression on her face.

"It's worthless, Dad," said Elizabeth, turning her attention back to the tape. She threw up her hands in the air. "This tape narrows the possibilities down to just about every man in the country."

"Well, we'll just play it through one more time," said Sam.

"Play it again, Sam!" Jessica quipped, drawing a

laugh from the group. Sam joined in the laughter as she rewound the tape a final time.

"It's so frustrating," said Mrs. Wakefield as the tape played through. "I can't make out his face at all through that bandanna."

"And the overcoat completely hides his clothing," said Sam.

"I can't even tell what color his hair is because of that felt hat," added Ned.

"There is simply not one possible clue!" exclaimed Elizabeth, falling back against the couch.

But while her family talked, Jessica was staring at the tape in shock, a sick feeling settling in the pit of her stomach. She didn't join in as the others expressed their frustration about their inability to identify the kidnapper. Because she did see a clue—a dead giveaway, in fact. The kidnapper wasn't wearing any gloves. And on the little finger of his left hand was the ring that Jessica had given him.

Who is Jeremy Randall really? Don't miss Sweet Valley High #111, **A Deadly Christmas**, *the terrifying conclusion to this riveting three-part miniseries.*

Bantam Books in the Sweet Valley High series
Ask your bookseller for the books you have missed

SIGN UP FOR THE SWEET VALLEY HIGH® FAN CLUB!

Hey, girls! Get all the gossip on Sweet Valley High's® most popular teenagers when you join our fantastic Fan Club! As a member, you'll get all of this really cool stuff:

- Membership Card with your own personal Fan Club ID number
- A Sweet Valley High® Secret Treasure Box
- Sweet Valley High® Stationery
- Official Fan Club Pencil (for secret note writing!)
- Three Bookmarks
- A "Members Only" Door Hanger
- Two Skeins of J. & P. Coats® Embroidery Floss with flower barrette instruction leaflet
- Two editions of *The Oracle* newsletter
- Plus exclusive Sweet Valley High® product offers, special savings, contests, and much more!

Be the first to find out what Jessica & Elizabeth Wakefield are up to by joining the Sweet Valley High® Fan Club for the one-year membership fee of only $6.25 each for U.S. residents, $8.25 for Canadian residents (U.S. currency). Includes shipping & handling.

Send a check or money order (do not send cash) made payable to "Sweet Valley High® Fan Club" along with this form to:

SWEET VALLEY HIGH® FAN CLUB, BOX 3919-B, SCHAUMBURG, IL 60168-3919

NAME _____
(Please print clearly)

ADDRESS _____

CITY_____ STATE _____ ZIP_____
(Required)

AGE _____ BIRTHDAY_____ / _____ / _____

**Your friends at Sweet Valley
High have had their world
turned upside down!**

**Meet one person with a power
so evil, so dangerous, that it
could destroy the entire world
of Sweet Valley!**

A Night to Remember, the book that starts it all, is followed
by a six book series filled with romance, drama and suspense.

Life after high school gets even *Sweeter!*

Jessica and Elizabeth are now freshmen at Sweet Valley University, where the motto is: Welcome to college — welcome to freedom!

Don't miss any of the books in this fabulous new series.

♥ College Girls #1	0-553-56308-4	$3.50/$4.50 Can.
♥ Love, Lies and Jessica Wakefield #2	0-553-56306-8	$3.50/$4.50 Can.
♥ What Your Parents Don't Know #3	0-553-56307-6	$3.50/$4.50 Can.
♥ Anything for Love #4	0-553-56311-4	$3.50/$4.50 Can.
♥ A Married Woman #5	0-553-56309-2	$3.50/$4.50 Can.
♥ The Love of Her Life #6	0-553-56310-6	$3.50/$4.50 Can.

- -

Bantam Doubleday Dell
Books for Young Readers

Bantam Doubleday Dell
Dept. SVU 12
2451 South Wolf Road
Des Plaines, IL 60018

Please send the items I have checked above. I am enclosing $_____ (please add $2.50 to cover postage and handling). Send check or money order, no cash or C.O.D.s please.

_____
Name

_____
Address

_____
City   State   Zip

Please allow four to six weeks for delivery.
Prices and availability subject to change without notice.   SVU 12 4/94

Watch for

That's right! Your favorite twins, Jessica and Elizabeth, are coming to TV and right into your living room each and every week!

Share all the fun and excitement of their high school romances, friendships and intrigues with each new, must-see episode!

Check your TV listings for day and time. And don't miss any of the great Sweet Valley High books—available at your local bookstore!

Bantam Doubleday Dell
Books For Young Readers

BFYR 103-7/9